Already she'd risked Star's life not once but twice!

"You should really bring Star closer so you can see better!" Lyssa exclaimed.

Christina shook her head as they heard hoofbeats coming up the trail below them. Star lifted his head, nostrils flaring and muscles quivering at the sound of the approaching horses.

Christina gulped, afraid to move. What if Star bolted and fell off the rock? He'd plunge to his death! Why had she allowed herself to do such a stupid thing, anyway?

Lyssa didn't turn to look at Christina. Her eyes were intent on the horses and riders. "Ease that choke hold on Star's rope," she said quietly. "He's got to trust you." Christina stood frozen as the riders went past underneath them, ready to leap in front of Star if he moved.

Christina wondered for the hundredth time if she'd temporarily lost her mind when she decided to bring Star there. She'd only been there for part of a day, and already she'd risked Star's life not once but twice!

Collect all the books in the Thoroughbred series

THOROUGHBRED Super Editions

Ashleigh's Christmas Miracle
Ashleigh's Diary
Ashleigh's Hope
Samantha's Journey

ASHLEIGH'S Thoroughbred Collection

Star of Shadowbrook Farm
The Forgotten Filly
Battlecry Forever!

* coming soon

THOROUGHBRED

STAR'S CHANCE

CREATED BY
JOANNA CAMPBELL

WRITTEN BY
ALICE LEONHARDT

HarperEntertainment
An Imprint of HarperCollinsPublishers

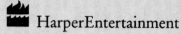

HarperEntertainment

An Imprint of HarperCollins*Publishers*

10 East 53rd Street, New York, NY 10022-5299

Produced by 17th Street Productions, an Alloy Online, Inc., company

HarperCollins books are available at special quantity discounts for bulk purchases for sales promotions, premiums, or fund-raising. For information please call or write: Special Markets Department, HarperCollins Publishers, 10 East 53rd Street, New York, NY 10022. Telephone: (212) 207-7528. Fax: (212) 207-7222.

ISBN 0-06-106669-9

HarperCollins®, 🔥®, and HarperEntertainment™ are trademarks of HarperCollins Publishers Inc.

Cover art © 2001 by 17th Street Productions, an Alloy Online, Inc., company

First printing: February 2001

Printed in the United States of America

Visit HarperEntertainment on the World Wide Web at
www.harpercollins.com

❖ 10 9 8 7 6 5 4 3 2 1

1

"WAKE UP, CHRIS," SAID ASHLEIGH GRIFFEN AS SHE PEERED into the darkened isolation stall at Whitebrook Farm. "Dr. Stevens is here. He just pulled into the driveway."

Sixteen-year-old Christina Reese blinked as she looked up at her mom, trying to make sense of where she was. As the cobwebs cleared in her brain, she realized that once again she'd fallen asleep in the stall, propped on a pile of bedding next to her chestnut colt, Wonder's Star. A second realization came to her, and Christina spun around to look at him. *Is he still okay?* she thought wildly.

As far as she could tell, he was. Star was standing peacefully next to her, dozing. What a difference from only a few weeks before, when he hadn't even had the strength to stand!

It seemed like forever since Star had gotten sick, though it had only been six weeks since Christina had first been aware that something was terribly wrong. It had started when Star was racing at Belmont and could barely finish the race. From there, he'd gone downhill fast. For a time it had even seemed as though he might die. But under the vet's supervision and with Christina's constant attention, Star had gone from being practically paralyzed to recovering completely.

Brushing herself off, Christina stood up and stretched the kinks out of her sore muscles. "Sorry, Mom. I know you don't like me to sleep in the barn. I didn't mean to. I was just so tired," she mumbled.

Ashleigh merely smiled. "Well, as soon as Dr. Stevens gives Star a clean bill of health, we're getting you back on a regular sleeping schedule," she said.

Christina turned a pleading eye to her mom. "He *is* all better, isn't he?" she asked softly.

Ashleigh opened the stall, nodding as she pulled off Star's blue-and-white sheet. "I think so. But let's wait until we have the official word from the vet."

Christina's head snapped up as she heard footsteps in the barn aisle. They grew louder as they approached the end stall, where the isolation area had been set up for Star. Her dad, Mike Reese, was walking next to the vet. Star's groom, Dani Martens, and George Ballard, Whitebrook's stallion manager, as well as Joe and Jonnie, two of Whitebrook's other grooms, followed them. Even Ian McLean, Whitebrook's head trainer, had taken time from the morning workouts to hear what Dr. Stevens had to say. Everyone on the farm had been cheering for Star, and now they wanted to be present to hear the good news.

Oh, please, let it be good news, Christina prayed silently.

"Morning, Chris," Dr. Stevens said, setting down his black bag. "You look like you got a good night's sleep."

Christina smiled weakly and pulled the straw out of her hair.

"Well, let me start off by saying that the blood samples I took the other day came back absolutely clean," Dr. Stevens said, stepping into the stall to examine Star.

"That's a good sign," Ashleigh said, reaching for Christina's hand.

Christina sucked in her breath, watching the vet intently as he went over every inch of Star's body.

"Hmmm," he said in that maddening way all vets have.

You're all better, you're all better, Christina chanted silently to herself as Dr. Stevens listened to Star's heartbeat. Her eyes were glued to the vet as he ran his hands over Star's topline and under his belly. Only two months before, Star's coat had been a glossy, fiery chestnut, but because of his mysterious illness it was now rough to the touch and lifeless.

Star snorted softly as the vet reached for the tube to thread up the colt's nostril so he could scope the animal's lungs.

"I'm sorry," Christina said, holding Star's nose. "I know you hate this."

"He's back on his feed in a big way, I hear," the vet said conversationally while he inserted the tube.

Christina nodded her head. "He's been licking his pan."

"Good, good," the vet said.

Christina waited anxiously. The examination was sure taking a long time. But she was glad Dr. Stevens was so thorough. Even though he'd been recommended by Brad Townsend, Star's former co-owner and Ashleigh's longtime nemesis, Christina and her family had been incredibly impressed by the dedication and skill with which he had treated Star.

At last Dr. Stevens straightened up and cleared his throat. "It's a miracle. It's a plain and simple miracle," he said, shaking his head.

Christina had been holding her breath, but now she let it out with an explosive, noisy whoosh. Star turned his expressive brown eyes in her direction. At another time the loud noise would have startled a highly sensitive Thoroughbred like Star, but he seemed to calmly accept the vet's pronouncement that he'd beaten the odds and returned from death's door as if it were the most natural thing in the world.

Christina was anything but calm. Fiercely she hugged her horse. "Did you hear that, Star?" she exclaimed. "You're all better!"

Up until now Christina had not dared to hope for a complete recovery. After all, it had been only a month since she'd sat with Star in this very stall, cradling his head in her lap, sure that any minute she was going to lose the horse she loved with all her heart. She felt as if a blacksmith's anvil had been lifted from her shoulders.

The vet shrugged, mystified. "His lungs are clear. His heart rate is normal. The blood work showed nothing. He's healthy as they come."

"And you still have no idea what was wrong with him?" Ashleigh asked the vet.

Dr. Stevens patted Star's shoulder as he turned to put his equipment back in its case. "I wish I did. I've never run so many tests without finding anything out. I went online with equine experts all over the world, and they're just as baffled as I am."

Mike shook his head and opened the stall door wide to let the vet out. "And as far as you know, only those two horses from Florida who were at Belmont with Star had whatever it was he had?"

"That's right," Dr. Stevens said. "And the autopsies on those two horses didn't turn up anything, either."

Christina shuddered as she considered the fact that Star could easily have died.

The vet smiled at her. "Well, one thing's for sure—I ought to write about Star's success story. Actually, it might be bad for business. It defies practical medicine."

"I knew he'd pull through," Dani said loyally to Christina. "After all, Star had you."

"And he has great spirit," added Ian.

"You showed them all, boy," Jonnie said, stepping in the stall to give Star a carrot.

Star munched matter-of-factly while he regarded his fan club.

Christina inhaled Star's special scent of hay and horse, her mind still overcome by relief. The nightmare was over. Star was all better. That was all that mattered.

And now that he was no longer sick, Christina could finally savor the sweet knowledge that Star was all hers! No longer did she have to give in to the whims of Brad Townsend and his horrible wife, Lavinia. Star would never have to endure the rough handling of Ralph Dunkirk, the Townsends' trainer. For Brad, convinced Star wouldn't make it, had agreed to let Christina buy out his share in Star at a ridiculously low price.

"Well, you *did* make it," Christina whispered triumphantly in Star's ear. "And what's more, we're going to make Brad really sorry he didn't believe in you!"

"What did you say, Chris?" Ashleigh asked, turning to her.

"Oh, nothing," Christina said quickly.

"Look at the two of them," Dr. Stevens said, chuckling. "They've got their own special language."

"That's for sure," Mike said. "You ought to see them on the racetrack. It's hard to tell where one leaves off and the other begins."

"Speaking of racing, I think the important thing right now is to take things a day at a time," cautioned Dr. Stevens. "Star needs to get his strength back, and then we'll see if he can run again. In the meantime, I don't see why you can't start riding him lightly. As far as breeding him at some point, well, we'll just have to wait and see."

Half listening, Christina turned to hug Star yet again. Closing her eyes, she didn't even notice when her mom and dad and the vet walked down the barn aisle. She was already miles away, mounted on her colt, thundering down the track at Churchill Downs. She could hear the roar of the crowd as she and Star rounded the clubhouse turn. She could feel his rippling muscles beneath her, his raw power and speed.

"As soon as you're fit again, we're going all the way to the Derby, boy," she whispered to Star. "We're going to show everyone how much spirit you really have. Can you smell those roses?"

Christina reached up to stroke Star's nose and look into the depths of his eyes. Suddenly she heard the clatter of a falling manure shovel, and she looked around to make sure no one was around to overhear her. If anyone knew what she was thinking, she'd never hear the end of it. As much faith as everyone had in Star, they wouldn't understand how she could even dare to dream about winning the Derby on him, not after what he'd been through.

It didn't matter that Star had some of the best breeding in the country or that his dam, Ashleigh's Wonder, had won the Kentucky Derby with an impressive time. It didn't matter how many important races he'd already won. He'd be running against the top two-year-olds in the country, but now he was back at square one, and he had less than six months to get back into condition.

"I know, it's not much time. But don't worry, big guy," Christina whispered into Star's ear. "Now that you're better, there isn't anything we can't do."

Wait till I tell Parker! she thought happily. She and Parker Townsend had been dating for a long time, much to his parents' annoyance. And though he had been training seriously for the Olympic three-day-event team, he'd taken time to check Star's progress and support Christina throughout the terrifying ordeal.

Frowning, Christina ran her hand through her hair and pursed her lips as she considered Star's thin frame. "We've got to get your muscle back. Now that you're officially better, I can start taking you for hacks. Nothing too strenuous. Just a little tooling around Whitebrook so you can see your friends again. How about that?"

Star regarded her quietly, as if considering her plans, then let out a soft whuffing sound. Christina leaned against him, knowing that she really had to get ready for school. She toyed with the idea of begging Ashleigh to let her skip it for once.

"Oh, Star, she'll never go for it," Christina muttered aloud. "Well, anyway, let's get you out of here. Say adios to the isolation stall. It's time to go back to your home sweet home."

Star nodded his finely chiseled head as if in agreement. After Christina replaced his sheet, she clipped his lead rope on his well-oiled halter and led him down the barn aisle, back to his regular stall.

Star sniffed his familiar surroundings appreciatively as Christina filled his flat-sided blue water bucket. She watched while Star sipped, sucking up the water through his whiskery lips.

"Time to trim your beard, too, I think," Christina said with a smile. How wonderfully luxurious it was to think about details such as whisker trimming again!

Glancing at her watch, Christina wrinkled her nose.

"Okay, I have to go to school now," she said reluctantly, latching the stall. "You relax and start thinking about how we're going to blow them all away on the track."

As she made her way back to the house, Christina felt so happy, she did something she hadn't done since Star had gotten sick: She ran all the way up to the door, laughing like a little kid.

"Well, what do you think?"

Christina jumped back. It was a few minutes before first period. She had just opened her locker at Henry Clay High School, and streamers, confetti, and small blue-and-white balloons had come tumbling out. On the locker door, someone had hung a sheet of white paper with the brightly painted words "Go Star!"

Christina turned to her friends, mystified. She'd only heard Dr. Stevens's pronouncement an hour before. How had they had the time to pull together such an elaborate gesture?

"I'm quick, aren't I, cuz?" said her cousin, Melanie

Graham, who was an apprentice jockey just like Christina. She had been living with Christina's family at Whitebrook ever since moving from New York almost four years ago. After a slightly rocky start, they were now close friends.

"You can say that again," said Kevin McLean, Ian's son, his green eyes sparkling as he shifted his weight from the knee he'd injured in a soccer game. "The minute my dad went down to the training oval and told everyone, Melanie raced to the barn phone and called practically everyone we knew."

"Actually, we've been planning it for days," confessed Katie Garrity, Christina's friend, who lived in town. "We knew it would all turn out okay. We were just waiting for the word."

Tears blurred Christina's vision. "You guys are so great," she said.

The bell rang, and everyone scattered for their first class. But Christina lingered, gazing at the balloons and her friends' message. It was funny, but seeing Star's recovery spelled out in writing in front of her was the final proof she needed. She could relax now. Everything was going to be all right again.

But as Christina started to walk to class and listened to her footfalls echo in the now empty school corridor, another thought pushed its way forward in her mind. She didn't have to worry about fighting for

Star's life anymore, but there was no point in kidding herself. It was going to take many months of hard work—and possibly even another miracle—if she and Star were ever going to race again, let alone win the Derby!

2

"THAT'S RIGHT, MR. SUN BUM, SOAK UP LOTS OF VITAMIN D," said Christina that afternoon as she approached the turnout where Star was dozing in the pale November sunshine.

The minute the bus had dropped Christina off after school, she'd charged into the house, jumped into her jeans, and raced down to the barn. She panicked when she saw Star's empty stall. Had he gotten sick during the day and been returned to the isolation stall?

But then she saw that Dani had written "Star, Paddock A, 2:30" on the chalkboard in the aisle.

"Good idea," Christina said approvingly. "After that layup, you need all the fresh air you can get."

She tilted her head upward and let the Kentucky sunshine warm her face. Off in the distance she could hear the hum of activity in the stable area. It was sweet and familiar, and Christina had missed it. Busy with Star, she had slacked off on her exercise riding and hadn't done much in the way of barn chores in the past few weeks.

Guiltily she thought of the Whitebrook horses she had always helped exercise-ride and race and the bay colt named Gratis she'd ridden for Vince Jones. The gruff trainer had had to find a replacement jock when she'd ducked out on him after Star got sick.

"Well, what else could I do?" Christina asked Star. "How could I ride anyone else when I had you to worry about?"

Star raised his elegant head and regarded Christina before reaching down for a clump of grass. "How can you be so calm?" she asked, marveling at how placid he seemed. "I'm so hyper I can barely stand still!"

Christina felt her throat close and her eyes fill. She'd never get over this incredible rush of feeling she experienced when she watched her horse doing ordinary things such as eating grass in a paddock. Star was alive! Star was well! And what was more, she was about to ride him for the first time in weeks.

"Not too much, though," Christina said as she grabbed Star's leather halter and lead, which were hanging on the gate. Slipping in between the rails, she placed the halter on her colt and led him back to the barn for a thorough grooming session.

"While you were out there catching the rays, I was catching all kinds of heat from Mr. Hamrick for rushing through my driver-ed quiz," Christina confided to Star as she clipped him into the crossties. "He kept saying, 'This just isn't like you, Ms. Reese.'"

Star snorted. And Christina added, "That's right. Who needs to drive when you can ride?"

Christina kept up a nonstop flow of talk while she lovingly caressed Star's scratchy coat with soft body brushes. She frowned as a few clumps of dead hair fluttered to the rubber flooring. The yellowish hairs looked nothing like Star's usual copper color.

"Not a problem. You just need vitamin supplements. A little oil," Christina chattered on. "Don't you give it another thought. A couple more visits to Christina's Grooming Salon, and your coat will look fabulous again, I guarantee it."

Star stood still as Christina finished her brushwork. He didn't move as she picked out his shapely hooves with a hoof pick and then placed the pads and saddle on his back. When she slipped his bridle over his poll, Star clamped his jaw, refusing to take the bit.

"Open up. I know it's been a while," Christina said, pressing her finger against the bar of his mouth. Finally Star accepted the bit.

"We're just about ready. You can't wait to get out

15

there, can you?" Christina crooned while she fastened the noseband and throatlatch.

Actually, Star didn't look eager to go out there at all. His eyes were half closed, and his lower lip drooped. Normally a highly bred racehorse who'd been confined to a stall day after day would be dancing in the grooming area, impatient to be off and expend all that pent-up energy.

"You *are* all better," Christina said firmly, looking worriedly into Star's eyes for reassurance before leading Star out of the barn. They were bright and unclouded.

Star jangled his bit, but other than that, he gave no sign that he'd even heard Christina.

Ashleigh poked her head out of the barn office as Christina and Star walked past. "Lyssa Hynde phoned a while ago, and I gave her the news about Star. She yelled so loudly, I figured the whole state of Montana must have heard her."

Christina grinned. She had only recently gotten to know Lyssa when she'd spent time in Lexington, but she had taken a liking to the off-the-wall girl right away. Country-girl Lyssa had been a local sensation when she had unexpectedly swept into Kentucky and beaten all the other contenders for the Olympic three-day-event equestrian team. Lyssa had been Parker's chief rival during the Olympic selection trials, and to add to the tension, while she was in Kentucky she had

16

stayed at Whisperwood Farm, where Parker worked and trained.

Parker hadn't liked Lyssa at first, claiming that her riding style was gimmicky and crude. That had caused some trouble between Christina and her boyfriend, because Christina herself had warmed immediately to Lyssa's innovative horsemanship. Christina had spent a great deal of time with Lyssa, and Parker hadn't liked it one bit. But soon Parker caved in, impressed by Lyssa's gentle but firm way of getting any horse to do whatever she asked. Now they were all fast friends and kept up regularly with each other—even though Lyssa was back at her ranch training her horse, Soldier Blue, for the Olympics.

"I can't wait to tell Lyssa how great it is to ride you again," Christina said to Star. In fact, Lyssa would understand why Christina refused to give up hope of racing Star in the Derby. She was just as ambitious as Christina was, maybe even more so.

Christina tickled the colt's ears and went over to the mounting block.

"That is definitely a happy sight," called Melanie, who'd just come down to the barn to start her barn chores. "Star power—restored!" She gave Christina a thumbs-up before disappearing into the feed room.

Christina knew her cousin was especially glad for her because they both had been dealing with bad luck lately: Christina with Star's sickness, and Melanie with the threat that Perfect Image, the horse she'd come to love, would be ripped away from her and sold to Brad Townsend. But recently luck had taken a positive turn for Melanie when Image had been allowed to come to Whitebrook for training. She'd been telling Christina over and over again that it was Christina's turn for a little good news. Finally that time had come.

"You go, girl!" called Maureen Mack, Whitebrook's assistant trainer, as she emerged from the weanling barn. She held up her clipboard in salute. Christina waved at Maureen, then climbed aboard Star's back, adjusting her stirrups so that they were longer than usual. She wouldn't be breezing that day, so she didn't need to have them up in racing position. She pursed her lips as she pulled up Star's girth one hole, and then another.

The thought *He really has lost weight* flashed through Christina's brain. Turning Star's head toward the paths leading past the broodmare pastures, she settled into her saddle. Before too long she became conscious of how sharp Star's withers seemed to be. Maybe she should have put on an extra pad, she thought.

Not a problem, Christina told herself. It was just another aspect of Star's recovery. She sank deep in her seat, encouraging Star to move out at a walk. "Now, I know you haven't been out in a long time, but we have to take it easy."

Star walked forward steadily, but without any real impulsion.

"Well, I didn't mean *this* easy," Christina said, laughing. She squeezed him forward, and they made their way along the rail of the paddock where several broodmares, including Miss America and Perfect Heart, were turned out. Both had recently weaned their foals and were grazing lazily.

"Check it out, girls," Christina called cheerily to the mares. "Look who's back!"

She watched the mares for a moment, then leaned down to pat Star. Cupping her hand over her eyes, she looked down toward the stallion barn and was amazed to realize that it looked so much bigger than before. When had the construction been completed?

Over the last few weeks she hadn't even realized that the long-talked-about expansion had finally become a reality.

"Yikes. I guess have some catching up to do," Christina said as she gently nudged Star forward with her heels. She made a mental note to ask her dad about the expansion. She knew it was important to him.

Christina felt content simply to sit on Star's back as he walked along. But as she continued, she was aware that Star was hardly going forward at all. *Plodding* was the word that best described his stride. She nudged him again. His only response was to lower his head a little.

"You tired already? Maybe we ought to head back," Christina said aloud.

Okay, it's no biggie, she thought, irritated at herself for feeling vaguely uneasy. *No need to overreact. If you'd been in bed forever with the flu or whatever, you probably wouldn't feel like kicking up your heels the first day out, either.*

Still, as she turned Star for home, she couldn't push down the feeling that it didn't feel like Star was tired, exactly; it was more like he was *disconnected* somehow. Maybe, Christina thought, she had been getting ahead of herself, galloping ahead mentally and thinking about the Derby—or even racing, for that matter. Maybe it was true what people had been saying, that all Star would be good for would be breeding—if that.

Oh, stop driving yourself nuts. It is his first day back, she reminded herself. *Give him a chance.*

The next day was Thursday, and when Christina saddled up Star and headed out for a short hack, she knew right away that nothing had changed. Star was just the way he had been the day before, distant and slow and somehow not in sync with her. He looked the same, but he was nothing like the old Star.

"All right," Christina said thoughtfully. "Now, how can I fix this?"

She paused, considering which of Whitebrook's many paths to take on their hack. Finally she decided on the one that started up behind the stallion barn.

"We haven't been up this way in a long time," Christina said, patting Star's neck. "I can get a closer look at the expansion, and you can check out some new scenery. Maybe that'll perk you up."

It didn't seem to make any difference to the colt which way Christina chose to go. He merely ambled along like an old school horse and didn't react in the slightest when he heard Terminator, Whitebrook's aggressive stallion, kicking ferociously at his stall wall.

"Hey, sweetie pie, you've got to snap out of it," Christina crooned a while later when they stopped on a hill overlooking the training oval. "Look, down there. It's your favorite place. Bet you can't wait to get out there and let it rip."

But it was pretty plain that Star didn't care where he was. He hardly glanced at the place where only a few months earlier he'd put in record-breaking works.

"Come on, boy, let's see some enthusiasm," Christina coaxed as they headed toward the meadow. "This has to be more fun for you than standing around your stall the way you have been. Come on. The leaves are dropping. Snow's just around the corner. There have got to be some good smells in the air. I know you. You love your hacks."

Christina knew she was trying to convince herself as much as Star. She might as well be sitting on hay bales and trying to ride them, for all the response she was getting from Star! Christina couldn't help thinking back to the times when Melanie had actually practiced her racing seat on a couple of bales and had named her "mount" Old Hay Bales.

"Hey, Hay Bales, has someone switched horses on me?" Christina joked. She leaned forward to rub Star's poll, but he gave no sign of having felt her touch.

"Okay, this isn't funny anymore," Christina said, frowning.

Just as they got to the meadow, Star stopped in his tracks.

"What is it, big guy?" Christina asked with surprise. Ordinarily Star was so obedient that he'd never do something such as stopping without being told to. She looked around to see what had caused Star to brake. Scanning the grassy area in front of her, however, Christina could see nothing.

"It's okay," Christina said soothingly to her horse. "See? No monsters here."

She squeezed with her heels and clucked, but Star didn't budge. It was as though he had no idea what she wanted.

"Let's go, Star," Christina said firmly.

Maybe something else was wrong, Christina reasoned. Hurriedly she dismounted and looked the colt over closely. She listened to his lungs for any telltale rattling and to his stomach for any suspicious rumblings that might mean he was colicking. Nothing. Then she ran her hands up and down his legs, feeling for swelling or heat. His legs were cool to the touch. Finally she picked up each hoof and examined it for rocks or anything else that might have caused discomfort.

"Tell me what's wrong," she pleaded worriedly.

A crazy thought popped into her mind. Maybe Star was having flashbacks to his days at Townsend Acres. Brad Townsend's head trainer, Ralph Dunkirk, had mistreated him, and it had temporarily altered his personality. Had something triggered those bad memories?

It couldn't be, Christina told herself firmly. She and Star had been inseparable for a long time now. They had come a long way together since those troubled days. Under her loving care, Star had transformed from acting suspicious and aggressive to being responsive and totally in tune with her. It had to be something else.

The sun was climbing higher in the sky, and Christina remounted. She bit her lip as she clucked, cajoled, and encouraged Star to move forward just one step. But he refused to budge.

"Come on," she said with a slight edge she couldn't help. She felt instantly guilty and followed up with more gentle words of encouragement. But she could see it was no use. Star had planted himself, and there was no way he was going forward.

"So are we going to stand here all day?"

It appeared that they just might. Star didn't move, except to shudder off a fly.

"Follow the *itancan*," Christina whispered to herself. That was something Lyssa had talked about during her sessions with Christina. She had explained that *itancan* was a Native American term for "leader." And while Lyssa wasn't big on forcing a horse to bend to a person's will, she did believe that once a person established herself as a worthy leader or *itancan*, the horse would naturally follow.

Only Star wasn't about to follow Christina's directions. He continued to stand, clearly not willing to accept Christina's leadership. After a few moments, scarcely believing it, Christina dismounted and tossed the reins over her colt's head. Then she turned away from the meadow and led Star back down the paths toward the barns.

"Oh, great," Christina muttered as, drawing closer, she spotted Melanie and Parker coming toward her.

"Hey, Chris, uh, you're supposed to be *on* the horse," Parker called out jokingly.

24

"That's the general idea," Melanie added, pushing her blond hair behind her ears.

Christina didn't respond, and they exchanged looks.

"Hey, is everything okay?" Parker said, switching from joke mode to serious.

Christina wrinkled her brow. "Yeah," she said, her voice shaking.

"Star's walking funny," Melanie observed. "Not lame, but *differently*."

"Like he's in slow motion," supplied Parker.

"There's nothing wrong," Christina snapped. "I mean, there's nothing *wrong* wrong. He's not limping or anything. But it's the weirdest thing. He just suddenly stopped at the meadow and refused to move."

Melanie's eyes scanned Star quickly. "Do you think he's sick again?"

Christina's stomach lurched at the thought. "No," she said quickly. "Look at him. His eyes are bright. I checked him all over. There's nothing wrong, I'm sure of it. But he's acting really weird. Sluggish, and like he's not really there."

"Bizarre," Melanie said, shaking her head.

Parker shrugged and thought for a moment, his handsome face a study in concentration. "You know, there's something my grandfather always told me."

Christina leaned forward. Parker's grandfather, Clay Townsend, was a famous horseman. Christina thought the world of him and took his words of wisdom seriously.

"Sometimes horses who've been sick are just like invalid people. They take a while mentally to catch up with the fact that physically they're okay now."

"That makes sense," exclaimed Christina. "But he wasn't sick *that* long. Do you really think he'd change so much?"

Melanie shrugged and started waving her hands the way she did when she got worked up about something. "Remember that story Lyssa told us about how Blue got struck by lightning and how she had to work with him after the burns healed? She said it caused so much emotional trauma, she had to start all over gentling him again."

Christina frowned.

"Maybe Star's got something like post-traumatic stress syndrome," Parker said. Seeing Christina's look, he added, "It's probably nothing that bad. Maybe it's just that he's gotten so used to feeling blah, he doesn't really realize that he's better."

Christina considered it. "Well, he *is* acting like he still thinks he's sick," she said, tugging on the reins again and continuing on toward the barn.

"I don't think you should worry about it, though," Melanie called after her.

"Give it time," Parker said, patting Star's hindquarters as they walked back to the stable area.

Christina rolled her eyes when she was sure her friends couldn't see her anymore. It was easy for them to brush off Star's strange behavior. But what if he stayed that way forever?

"All right, boy, time to show everybody that you're back and better than ever," Christina said the next day as she picked up the reins. It was early, but as usual, Whitebrook was already bustling with activity.

Christina had been determined to get back to her regular routine and had already exercised several horses that morning. But she hadn't been able to think about anything besides how to get Star out of his funk. She'd been grateful when Melanie offered to ride her last assigned horse for her, and she'd dashed immediately for Star's stall.

Now, clucking softly, she cued him forward. The two turned toward the path leading up to the broodmare turnouts. "We're going back up to the meadow," Christina said aloud. "And today we're going to walk right through it."

Star flicked one ear back but didn't seem to have an opinion.

"Good, then it's settled." Christina sat deeper in her saddle, taking a long breath of cool morning air. She forced herself to look around and enjoy the scenery a little. If Star needed to realize that he was all better, Christina reasoned, then she needed to act as if everything was completely normal again.

But it wasn't normal at all. They hadn't gone more than a few short yards when Christina became aware that she was driving Star with every step. She listened to his breathing, but there was nothing labored about it, and he wasn't off his stride. Physically he was fine; his head just wasn't into it.

"Let's go, big guy," Christina murmured uneasily. "Pretend we're back at Belmont and we've just spotted an opening. We're going to make our move—now!"

But Star acted as if she weren't even there. *Well, at least he's moving,* Christina tried to tell herself. "But no stopping," she said aloud.

This day, however, Star didn't wait till he got to the edge of the meadow. Just as they made their way past the first broodmare pasture, Star planted his hooves and halted.

"Not this time," Christina said under her breath, immediately giving him a sharp nudge. Nothing. It was as if Star didn't feel a thing. He merely switched his tail.

"Come on," she said in a loud voice.

She continued urging him forward, all the while looking for real reasons that Star might be hesitating. There just weren't any. Christina used every riding technique she'd ever learned to encourage the chestnut to move out. But try as she might, nothing Christina did could make Star take another step.

After several minutes, fighting tears of frustration, Christina slumped and gave up. Then she slid off and ran the stirrup irons up the leathers. *He needs more time*, she chanted inwardly with each footfall as she led Star back to the barn.

"Maybe we should have Dr. Stevens look at him again," she said to her mother after she'd groomed Star and put him away.

Ashleigh looked up from the schedules she was working on at her desk, her eyes full of concern. "I know that Star's pretty rusty after his illness, but you just have to be patient and work through it," she said.

"Work through it? I can hardly get Star to walk," Christina grumbled.

Just then the phone rang, and Ashleigh raised a finger to indicate she wouldn't be on more than a minute. Christina mouthed, "We'll talk later, when you're not busy," and left the office. There was no point in pursuing the conversation. Ashleigh didn't understand that it was more than a matter of Star's being a little rusty.

• • •

"Could it be that you're not being tough enough?" Parker asked later that night.

"I can't be any tougher," Christina replied, toying with the phone cord. Glancing at a photo of Star in the winner's circle at a recent race, she frowned. "You know how sensitive Star is."

"Well, that's true," Parker said. "I guess it's a matter of figuring out what's going on in his head. But I wonder if maybe you're babying him these days."

Rather than argue, Christina switched the subject, asking Parker about his mare, Foxy, and how their training was going. After all, his Olympic dream was just as important to him as Star and the Derby were to her.

After she hung up with Parker, Christina sprawled on her bed, idly looking out the window at the night sky. It was easy to shrug off what Parker said because it stung, but maybe he was right, she thought uncomfortably. Maybe because Star had been so sick, she had gotten into the habit of letting him off the hook too easily. All her years around Thoroughbreds had taught her that though it definitely took kindness, it also took firmness to bring out the best in the hot-blooded breed.

Rising early the next morning, Christina resolved that she'd be firmer with Star if he acted up again. She went to the barn and groomed the colt, talking to him all the while.

"No funny stuff today," she said with determination as she placed the pads and saddle on his back. "I know you're better. It's time to get back to work if we're going to get you in shape in time for the Derby." She kissed Star on his velvety muzzle and looked pleadingly into his eyes. "You do want to race again, don't you?"

Today Christina pointed Star in the direction of Whitebrook's long gravel drive. She would try hacking him along the paths that were set back behind the main road, avoiding the meadow altogether.

"So far so good," Christina crooned while they went past the parking area. All the while she tried not to notice Star's plodding pace. At least he was moving.

It wasn't until they neared Whitebrook's plain black mailbox that the trouble started. Star dug in his heels, a move that Christina was becoming all too familiar with.

"Oh, no you don't," she said stubbornly, squeezing his sides with her heels.

Star's ears swiveled away, signaling that he wasn't paying attention to her. Hating herself as she did so, Christina dug her heels sharply into his sides. Ordinarily such a move would send a sensitive horse forward like a shot. But now it only served to make Star bunch his muscles and hunch his back.

"I don't want to fight you," Christina said, exasperated.

She turned him in a circle. Star moved sullenly, but when she tried to get him to go forward again, he refused.

"I'm not giving up today," she said in a tight voice. "I am *not* climbing off and wimping it back to the barn."

Several more tense minutes passed. Christina bit her lip in concentration, alternating her aids and circling. But just when she thought she might be breaking through to Star, he suddenly coiled like a spring and erupted into a series of sharp bucks. Christina was so surprised, she fell forward onto his neck and lost a stirrup, but she quickly regained her seat.

"What has gotten into you?" she gasped, flabbergasted.

Whirling again, Star faced the main stable area, where Christina saw Parker's truck. He must have just pulled in. Out of the corner of her eye, she saw Parker's tall frame as he stepped out of his pickup.

"Like I need an audience," she muttered, fighting to keep her seat. "Oh, Star, please don't do this," she moaned, pulling his head up so that he couldn't buck again. He shook his head, trying to evade the bit, and then whirled again. The whirling continued until Christina was dizzy. Finally she slid off, dismayed and furious.

"Don't say it," she said, leading Star past Parker. "I tried being tough. It's not working."

Parker shook his head as he turned to walk alongside her. "There's nothing to say, I guess, except that I see what you mean. Wow."

Christina took off her helmet and shook her hair out. Gratefully she handed the reins to Dani when the groom ran forward to meet her by the training barn.

"You two look like you were in a train wreck," Dani said, her eyes wide as she took in Star's sweat-stained, dusty coat. "Everything okay?"

Christina nodded and turned away, tears blinding her. Parker put his arm around her shoulders, but he didn't speak until they were well across the stable yard. Then he turned her to face him, his smoky gray eyes dark with concern.

"I know you're upset," he said. "But we'll figure this out."

Christina wiped her eyes with her sleeve. "It's just so totally unlike him. Everyone tells me to give it time, but he's changed. It's as if he doesn't know me. I don't think giving him time will do a thing."

"He's changed, all right," Parker said slowly.

"I should go back and groom him," Christina said abruptly.

"Let Dani do it. You need to cool off. We've got to think this through."

"As if I've been thinking about anything else," Christina said with a sigh. She kicked viciously at a clod of dirt.

"Know what I think?" Parker asked. "I was thinking that maybe Star needed a change of scenery to clear his head. What I really think is—uh, you ready to hear it?"

"Of course I am."

Parker was silent for a moment. Then he blurted, "Star should leave Whitebrook."

Christina pulled out her ponytail holder and shook her hair so that it fell around her shoulders. "Now how would that help? Star's been all kinds of places in the past few months. How will it make a difference if I take him to a racetrack?"

Parker met her eyes. "I'm not talking racetracks. Actually, I think a racetrack is probably the last place Star needs to go to right now. I'm talking about something completely different." He took a deep breath and added, "Montana."

Christina snorted. "Stop joking around." But then, seeing Parker's look, she sputtered, "Where did that come from? You want us to hitchhike there, and tell whoever's driving, 'Hey, dump me off at the state line. My horse hasn't been here before, and he wants to take a look around?'"

Parker shook his head. "I'm serious. You should take Star to Lyssa's ranch."

Christina gaped at Parker. "Parker Townsend, I think you've been training too much."

"No, hear me out," Parker pressed on. "Remember all those stories Lyssa told us about healing horses? Maybe she could work her magic on Star."

"Lyssa's a great rider, and she's done wonders with Blue, but . . . Star?" Christina protested. "He's got to get ready to race. I can't go hauling him off across the plains to learn how to be a—a *cow*horse. In case you forgot, Lyssa's ranch is a dude ranch. People pay to go there and play cowboy."

Parker looked pointedly up by the mailbox where Star had just exploded. "Star doesn't look like he wants to get ready to race," he said with finality. "Just think about it, okay?" he added, turning and heading for his pickup.

Christina watched him go. "I am thinking about it," she shouted after him. "And I'm thinking that you are absolutely nuts!"

"Parker? Parker, wait up!"

It had just occurred to Christina how snotty she sounded. After all, Parker was only trying to help. She'd asked for his advice, and then every time he suggested something, she shut him down. Some girlfriend she was!

Catching up to him before he got into his truck and drove away, Christina slipped her hand inside his elbow to stop him. "Sorry. I didn't mean to act like such a jerk."

"But you *still* think I'm crazy, don't you?" Parker grinned. "That's fine. Lots of people do, you know."

Christina shook her head. "Parker, it's really sweet of you to try to help," she said. "But charging off to some half-wild—I can't take a risk like that."

Parker's laugh floated across the stable yard. "Don't give me that. Since when have you been afraid to take a risk?"

"I just don't think Montana's the answer."

"Why not?" Parker challenged. "Give me two good reasons."

"Well, for one, Star's home is here at Whitebrook—" Christina began.

Parker broke in. "C'mon, Chris. I didn't say *move* to Montana. I meant *visit*."

Christina gave him a look. "And for another, Montana's pretty far away."

"Ever hear of a horse van?" Parker shot back. "I'm telling you, Star could use the change of scenery, and I think Lyssa could help you guys."

Christina sighed. "I said it before. I don't agree with you."

Parker shook his head. "And you don't think it's strange that even though Star's acting totally bizarre, you won't try the one thing that might be just what he needs to get back on track?"

There was no use arguing with Parker. *Really,* she thought with annoyance, *he can be so stubborn sometimes!*

"Forget it, will you? Star and I are staying right here in Kentucky!"

With that, Christina spun around and headed back

to the barn, irritated with Parker for being so persistent, but more annoyed at herself for being such a jerk once again to someone whose heart was in the right place. Her problems with Star were really getting to her!

Dani had just finished rinsing Star with warm water when Christina stomped into the grooming area. Dani glanced at Christina and started removing the excess water with a scraper.

"Thanks, Dani, you're a lifesaver," Christina said in a tight voice, holding out her hand. "I can finish up now."

"Sure thing." Dani handed over the scraper and paused before picking up the full bucket next to her.

"You okay, Chris?" the groom asked with concern.

Christina nodded, and Dani paused before turning to slosh the rest of the water down the drain. Dani looked as though she was about to ask another question, but she closed her mouth and rubbed Star's dripping muzzle instead.

With a wink at Christina, Dani stage-whispered to Star, "It's time to cool it with the bad-boy antics, sweetie. I think you've given Chris enough to worry about lately."

Then she tilted her ear toward Star's muzzle, as if listening to the big colt's reply.

Turning to Christina, Dani added, "Your problem's

solved. You see, I speak horse. He says he'll be on his best behavior from now on."

With that, Dani walked down the barn aisle, swinging the bucket.

Christina sighed. *As if it were that easy!*

Running the scraper over Star's back and hindquarters, Christina squeezed out every last drop of water. No way was she going to chance putting him away damp and having him catch a cold on top of everything else.

Afterward Christina grabbed one of the large, fluffy towels that were folded and stacked neatly by her grooming box. When he was completely dry, she unclipped him from the crossties.

"Hey, Chris, forget what I said. It's not worth fighting about. It was just a wild suggestion, and I won't bring it up again. Scout's honor."

Christina turned around and saw Parker coming down the aisle, smiling and holding up two fingers in a gesture of peace. *Why did he come back?* she wondered. Shrugging, she turned to snap on Star's lead rope.

"Fine," she said. "Consider it forgotten."

As Christina started to lead Star off the rubber mat, he pulled back, ripping the rope out of her hand and tearing two of Christina's fingernails well below the quick. Forgetting her pain as Star bumped his hindquarters on the padded wall, Christina leaped to catch the rope. Suddenly Star sprang forward, almost running her over and grazing Parker's foot. Christina held the lead rope tightly and brought him to a halt.

"Whoa," she said, stroking Star's neck, her heart beating wildly.

Parker examined the scrape Star's aluminum shoe had made on the toe of his shoe. "Good thing these are my practice boots," he said, tapping Star's muzzle. "You'd better grow up before you hurt someone, boy. You're acting like a weanling."

Christina bit back frustrated tears. "Easy, big guy. Come on," she said, tugging on the rope more gently this time.

Pulling Star along like the reluctant weanling Parker had joked about, Christina could practically feel her boyfriend's eyes tattooing "I told you so" into her back.

"Well, I'd better take off. Big lesson with Samantha this morning. I'll pick you up tonight at eight," he called after her.

Christina was confused. "Eight?" she echoed, turning to look at Parker over her shoulder.

"The party my parents are throwing for that prince from wherever who wants to breed his mares to our new stallion. Remember? I promised my parents I'd show up."

"Oh, that's right." Christina had almost forgotten. Parker didn't spend much time with his difficult parents, especially at their high-society events. She'd told him a couple of weeks earlier that she would come along and lend moral support.

She was reluctant to spend an evening with Brad and Lavinia, but she'd go through with it somehow. But she fervently hoped word hadn't drifted back to Brad about how strangely Star had been acting. It would be just like Brad to make a crack about how she'd blown her money buying out his half interest.

Don't be ridiculous, Christina told herself, putting Star away in his stall. *Brad's probably already forgotten about Star now that he's got Celtic Mist prepping for the Derby.* If he even thought about Star at all, he'd probably already written him off as a half-dead has-been.

As she and Parker pulled up in front of Townsend Acres, Christina felt her stomach tighten. Although the breeding farm was one of the most gorgeous and luxurious spreads in Kentucky, Christina had never felt quite right there. She much preferred cozy, rustic Whitebrook.

Stepping out of Parker's truck, Christina could already hear the classical music and brittle laughter wafting out the door. Glancing toward the main house

41

lit up with twinkly lights, she took a deep breath. She'd much rather be hanging out with Star in the warmth of his stall.

"Hey, check it out. Looks like the prince brought an army of bodyguards with him," Parker whispered in her ear, nudging and pointing. "Even my mom's ballroom isn't big enough for all those guys. If all the guests she sent out invitations to show up, there won't be any room for the band!"

Christina spotted a line of men wearing dark suits standing stiffly next to a row of black limousines that were parked at the entrance to the parking area. Several more stood discreetly behind the potted plants that flanked the grand front steps.

"Some of them are pretty cute," Christina teased.

"Right," Parker murmured. With that he squeezed Christina's hand and they made their way up the steps. Christina shivered as she heard one of the bodyguards murmur their names into a small mike clipped into his lapel as they passed.

Lavinia and Brad were standing with the prince at the front door, greeting their guests. As usual, Lavinia was dressed to the nines, this time in a shimmery black dress that clung to her figure. Her hands glittered with diamonds, and her voice was rich and silky as she proudly introduced her friends to her royal guest.

She and Brad are something, thought Christina, watching the way Parker's parents gushed over the introductions. It was still hard to believe Parker was their son. She glanced over at him as he straightened his tie and winked at her. He was doing his best, even though Christina could tell he'd rather be somewhere else, too.

"Oh, there you are, Parker," Brad said coolly. He drew Parker away from Christina toward the prince. "Prince Hamel, may I present my son, Parker Townsend. He's been short-listed for the United States Olympic equestrian team."

Conscious of being dismissed, Christina stepped back and watched as Parker spoke with the prince. Prince Hamel was a tall, middle-aged man with a regal bearing. He exchanged pleasantries with Parker, then looked past him at Christina. His eyes invited her to join them.

"And who is this?" he asked Lavinia with unfailing good manners.

Christina could tell Lavinia didn't like it one bit as she forced a smile.

After shaking hands with the prince and inquiring about his horses, Christina moved through the foyer with Parker toward the cavernous living room Lavinia called the ballroom.

"He seems like a good guy," Christina said.

Parker nodded. "Yeah. He's got quite a stable, I hear. Dad thinks his broodmares' lines could mix well with our stallions' lines. Wait right here. I'll go get us some soda."

Christina watched as Parker made his way through the crowd toward the table with a towering horse ice sculpture in the center. She turned to speak with a woman on her right. Too late she recognized the woman as a society reporter from the local newspaper.

"Isn't the prince the most handsome thing ever?" the woman said, brushing off Christina's polite greeting, her eyes scanning the room. "Oh, is that Talia Merriman? I must congratulate her on that colt she bought at the auction last week."

Christina had to bite the inside of her cheek to keep from laughing. She had heard that Mrs. Merriman had paid way too much for that particular colt in order to make a name for herself in Lexington racing society. Much as Christina loved the racing world, sometimes it could be ridiculous. There were always people who were attracted more by the glitz and glamour than by a true love of horses.

Across the room, she saw that Parker had been cornered by a couple of racing bigwigs. He flashed her an I'll-be-right-there look. Christina smiled thinly and was about to step out onto the balcony for some fresh air when Brad appeared at her elbow.

"I've been hearing all about your little troubles with Star," he said. He sipped from his crystal champagne flute and lifted his lips into a twisted grin.

Christina froze. How could he have he heard anything? Surely Parker hadn't—

"No, it wasn't Parker," Brad added, as if reading her mind. "But I have my ways."

Christina lifted her chin. "I'm sure you do, but I can't imagine why you care. You wrote Star off as dead and sold your share of him to me, remember?"

Brad smiled again without any warmth. "Best business decision I ever made. He may be recovered from his sickness, but from what I'm hearing, Star will never race again."

"That's not true!" sputtered Christina.

Brad lifted one of her hands and looked at her palm. "Hmmm. What are these, blisters?" He turned her hand over. "Broken nails? Too much hand-walking, I venture to guess. Too bad you're not actually *riding* Star much these days. I believe it's much easier to win a race that way."

Christina jerked her hand away from Brad, who adjusted his black bow tie and dusted a fleck off his tuxedo jacket.

"You're wrong. Star might be having trouble coming back from what he's been through, but he's going to come back. I promise you, you'll regret selling your share to me!" she said with a flash of anger.

Brad chuckled and raised his champagne glass in salute. "Brave words, Christina Reese, nothing more. Let me give you a little advice: Your parents have bred many other promising Thoroughbreds. Why don't you put your energy into them and forget about Star? You're wasting your time."

With that he turned his back to her and disappeared into the crowd.

Instantly Parker appeared at her side. "What did my dad say to you?"

Christina shook her head and bit her lip. Then she turned to Parker and looked him in the eye. "Take me home as soon as you can. I want to call Lyssa right away!"

"No," Ashleigh said, setting a teapot full of hot water on the kitchen table. "I know it's not going well with Star right now, but I think taking him to Montana is a little extreme."

Christina leaned forward. "I thought that exact same thing when Parker first suggested it to me. I know it sounds off the wall. But Mom, Star's a mess, and I'm desperate."

Ashleigh shook her head and sat down, idly dropping a tea bag into the pot. She glanced up at the window, where raindrops were spattering against the pane. "I'm just not sure that taking him all the way to Montana would be worth the strain on his system. There's the travel and adjusting to a new climate and everything."

"Parker thinks it'll really do him some good."

Christina hoped that mentioning Parker's name might persuade her mom. After all, now that Parker was an Olympic contender, surely Ashleigh would take his suggestions seriously. But Ashleigh merely poured her tea, then turned to a pile of papers that she was working on and sighed.

Christina turned to plead with her dad. She knew she'd have to get one parent on her side if she was going to make any headway. "Come on, Dad. If things keep going the way they are with Star, there's no telling what's going to happen."

Mike drummed his fingers on the table.

Christina pressed on. "Lyssa has a way with horses. You said so yourself. Maybe she can help me get through to Star."

Christina watched as Ashleigh's eyes met Mike's across the table.

"We've been telling you all along that it's just going to take time," her dad said after a long pause.

Christina bit her lip. There was no way she could tell her parents that she was running out of time. She couldn't tell them she was even thinking about trying to get Star ready for the Derby. They still seemed to believe they'd be lucky if they could use Star for breeding one day. "If I keep going like this and making zero progress, how is it going to help Star? Anyway, I really don't have anything to lose."

Mike tapped his temple thoughtfully. "She does have a point."

Sensing that her dad was weakening, Christina burst out, "I've done everything I can, and nothing I do makes any difference. Star's just not himself. If I don't do something quickly, I'll lose him forever."

She didn't add, *And Brad will have won.*

Ashleigh wrapped her hands around her mug of tea. "Well, Lyssa's accomplishments do sound pretty impressive."

Mike nodded. "Maybe it's worth a shot," he said slowly.

Ashleigh set down her mug. "The thing is, Chris, you have commitments here. I mean, we can ask someone to cover for you for your exercise rides, but what about school? You can't go charging off to Montana in the middle of the school year. It's your senior year."

Christina rolled her eyes. "I'm not planning to stay there forever. Thanksgiving vacation is coming up, and I could plan the trip around that. You know I've always been good about my schoolwork. My teachers

48

won't mind if I miss a few days as long as I make up my work."

"There are a few other considerations," Mike jumped in. "Like how will you transport Star there, and will Lyssa's mom and dad be okay with an extra guest showing up on their doorstep, and—"

"I don't know all the details yet, but I have to try," Christina cut in. "Please. I really believe it's Star's last hope."

There was a silence during which Christina became aware of the ticking of the kitchen clock. She held her breath.

Finally Ashleigh's shoulders slumped and she raised her hands. "I surrender. Call Lyssa. If it's okay with her family, I guess you could give it a go."

Christina jumped up and hugged her parents. "Thank you," she burst out breathlessly. Then she tore up to her room to call Lyssa.

"Lyssa, it's me, Christina Reese," said Christina breathlessly when Lyssa answered the phone.

"Hi, Chris!" Lyssa said. "I was so glad to hear that Star's all better."

"Uh, thanks," said Christina, all of a sudden feeling the enormous size of the favor she was about to ask Lyssa. *Anything for Star,* she thought, and pressed on. "Actually, it's because of Star that I'm calling."

"Is anything wrong?"

"Well, no," said Christina. "I mean, yes. He's all better physically, but he's just not the same horse. It's like we don't talk anymore. And, well, I have this idea...."

"Of course you're welcome here," Lyssa exclaimed when Christina finished blurting out the whole story. "As we say, 'Come on down anytime!' We have a fresh batch of city slickers coming in a few days, but there's always room for one more."

Christina heaved a sigh of relief. *So far so good.* But then she frowned. "There is one thing I have to work out: transportation. I only have my learner's permit, so I can't drive out there all alone. I could try to book a commercial van, but it's so last-minute."

"Hmmm," Lyssa said, considering the problem. Suddenly she whooped. "Hey, my uncle Cal and aunt Gwen are driving the rig through Ohio right now. They're hauling some Herefords and a pony that they bought, but there still oughta be room. I don't see why they can't swing south a bit and pick up you and Star."

Christina felt tears well up behind her eyes. "Would they do that?" It was too good to be true!

"Let me hang up with you and radio them right now. I just know we can work this out."

A few minutes later Christina set the phone back in its cradle and, instead of feeling thrilled that everything was falling into place, felt her heart plunge to her knees. She had just made plans to load up her beloved

50

Star and take him to a strange place. Who knew what could happen out there?

Shaking her head, Christina thought back to when she'd called Parker nuts. But she was the one who was nuts. After all, she had followed his advice and was about to do the craziest thing she'd ever done in her life!

4

"STAR? HEY, BIG GUY, YOU ALL SET?"

It was two days later, and Christina had just loaded Star in Lyssa's uncle's battered ten-horse trailer, which Star would ride in for two days while they traveled. Opening the small side door, she planted a kiss on Star's muzzle and adjusted the hay net that was in front of him. Lowering her voice, she added, "I know it's not like the deluxe vans you're used to, but it's roomy and I think you'll be comfortable. And look— you have some traveling buddies."

Star's nostrils puffed in and out as he sniffed the two red heifers and the gray Welsh pony in the trailer next to him.

Christina stifled a giggle. What must be going

through his mind? She could just picture him thinking, *What funny-looking racehorses!*

But Star didn't seem to care who his traveling companions were. After his initial inquiring snuffles, he turned back to his hay net and nibbled halfheartedly.

Watching Star's half-closed eyes, Christina bit her lip. Normally the colt would arch his neck and paw and snort in anticipation when he was loaded into a van. After all, to him, trailers meant racetracks. But now he stood, scarcely moving. Christina rubbed his ears, fighting the impulse to unload the big colt and forget the whole crazy idea of hauling him to Montana.

I'll just call Lyssa and tell her it was a bad idea, Christina thought wildly. *I'll tell her uncle Cal and aunt Gwen to take Star out and put him back in his stall right here where he belongs.*

She looked around the stable area, but then her eyes rested on the spot by the mailbox where just two days earlier Star had acted up. The dirt was still churned up where he had whirled and spun.

"No," she muttered as she started toward the truck, where Cal and Gwen Sayer were waiting. "I've got to go through with this."

"Got everything?" Cal asked. "We'd better get on the road. Daylight's turning into darkness."

The thin, older man adjusted his battered cowboy

hat and turned the key in the ignition. The engine coughed to life, and the truck vibrated so much that Christina wondered if a fender might fall off.

Christina nodded, not trusting herself to speak. She climbed up into the cab next to Gwen and looked out the window silently as the old rig made its way down Whitebrook's long drive. There was no one there except a few cavorting weanlings running alongside the paddock fence to see them off. Christina's mom and dad had left right after the morning works for an auction in Lexington. Everyone else was busy with barn chores.

"Call us when you arrive," Ashleigh had said before they left for the auction. Her tone had been casual, but Christina had seen the worry in her eyes.

Dani had solemnly handed Christina a shiny apple. She didn't look too happy about Star's heading west.

"I know you'll be good out there," she had said, pulling Star's ears affectionately. "We had that little talk. Remember? And stay away from snakes and rabbit holes and coyotes and bears. I hear Montana's full of them."

Christina had thanked Dani for the apple but wished the groom hadn't mentioned snakes and coyotes. For that matter, she wished Melanie hadn't brought up Montana's bear population the night before, either. She hadn't slept all night.

Too late to worry about bears, Christina thought. She

set her textbooks and laptop down at her feet in the crowded cab. The rig coughed and sputtered its way toward the main highway.

Lyssa's aunt Gwen, a large lady dressed in a loosely fitting blouse appliquéd with horses' heads, reached over and patted Christina's jean-covered knee.

"We're so happy to have you with us. You'll love the Black Thunder, I promise," she said warmly. "You've never been to Montana, have you?"

Christina shook her head. "I looked at the brochures that Lyssa sent me, though. The ranch looks so pretty."

"Oh, it is," Gwen assured her. "Though it could use a little money for fixing up."

Cal snorted as he glanced at his wife. "It's fancy enough as it is. Now that we have guests coming regularly, we've got all the trimmings."

Gwen said in a low voice to Christina, "You ignore him. He thinks indoor plumbing is the trimmings."

Was there indoor plumbing? Christina swallowed hard. She'd been so caught up in her concern for Star, she hadn't considered that the Black Thunder might be more rustic than she'd bargained for. But then she remembered the modern bathrooms she'd seen in the brochure. Closing her eyes, she mentally went through the brochure again, starting with the headline: HOWDY! MAKE YOURSELF AT HOME AT THE BEST DUDE RANCH IN THE WEST.

There was the main house with its Western interiors featured on the front cover, along with the long, unpainted horse barn. Inside there had been glossy photos of grizzled cowboys helping fresh-faced city folks "enjoy the Big Sky Country experience." Christina had been particularly interested in the pictures of Lyssa barrel-racing on Blue and leading children on ponies across rapid-running rivers. The other activities didn't look so bad, either: round-ups, campfires, wagon rides, barbecues, ranch crafts . . .

Okay, so it will be kind of like going to Camp Saddlebrook, Christina told herself. It had been a few years, but Christina still remembered the fun she had had camping out with her friends when she had spent three weeks at riding camp. She'd just pretend this was another trip to camp.

Unfortunately, it wasn't easy to forget that this time there was a whole lot more at stake.

"And don't you worry about that horse of yours, either. Our Lyssa can jump on a mountain lion and turn it into a show horse," Cal cut into her thoughts, laughing at his own joke.

Christina nodded, feeling a lump rise in her throat. Now that they were on the main road, she realized she was really doing it. She was leaving Whitebrook and her familiar routine. She was leaving her family and friends and taking Star thousands of miles away, where mountain lions and bears were commonplace.

I'm doing it for Star, she reminded herself.

Suddenly the trailer started rattling even louder, and Christina darted a nervous glance at the side mirrors. Was Star okay? she wondered.

Cal's eyes caught Christina's worried ones in the mirror, and they crinkled up into a grin.

"You look like you're wound up a little too tightly. Relax," he said to her. "This old trailer might be short on looks, but it's brought many a horse down many a road safe and sound."

Christina tried not to think about the number of times Lyssa had had to fight with the old truck to keep it going when she'd been in Kentucky preparing for Deer Springs. In fact, it had broken down at Whisperwood the morning she was to leave for a very important three-day event. But somehow her parents' friend Tor, who owned Whisperwood with his wife, Samantha, had managed to resurrect it from the dead.

But so far the truck was running smoothly, and soon she found herself relaxing and listening to the soothing lyrics of the country music coming from the dusty radio. After a while she stared out the window at the green Kentucky fields rolling past. Soon the past few sleepless nights caught up with her, and she slept, her cheek resting against the cold window.

She became aware that someone was patting her

shoulder, and she opened her eyes, trying to quickly adjust to the darkness.

Gwen was applying lipstick in the rearview mirror. "Cal will stop and stretch the horses' legs every few hours. Other than that, he likes to make tracks." She leaned closer and whispered conspiratorially, "But I told him that we were stopping and feeding you properly along the way."

As if she could eat! Christina's stomach was knotted, but she smiled gratefully at Gwen's kindhearted words.

She had to admit that the turkey sandwich they bought at the truck stop smelled incredibly good. She could feel her mouth watering as she unloaded Star and checked his legs. They were cool and firm. Walking him alongside Uncle Cal and the gray pony, she was surprised to find that she was pretty hungry after all. After they loaded up and pulled back onto the highway, Christina wolfed down her entire sandwich.

"That was great," she said, surprised at her appetite.

"These old truck stops have pretty decent food," Gwen said. "Not as good as Lyssa's mama's cooking, mind you, but adequate enough."

After a few hours Christina slept again, waking up briefly when Gwen took her turn behind the wheel.

"Cal needs his beauty sleep," she said to Christina.

Christina drifted off again and woke up just before

dawn after a terrifying dream of Star getting away from her and running in the opposite direction down the road. She was all dressed up to race, but she couldn't get the bridle on him.

The sun was a sliver on the horizon, and in the pink light, Christina could see the highway stretching endlessly in front of them, flanked on either side by tall cornfields. "Welcome to Iowa," Gwen said as she stopped the rig at a turnoff area.

Unloading Star, Christina undid his traveling wraps and checked his legs again for any swelling. She was happy to see that they still showed no signs of stocking up.

"Well, what do you think, boy?" she asked as she led him around the dusty turnoff area. Her eyes scanned the cornfields that seemed to stretch on forever. She shivered as a gust of cool wind hit her. "We're not in Kentucky anymore, that's for sure."

Star ambled along at the end of the lead rope, and Christina tried not to notice how dull his pace was compared to the pony's. After being cooped up in a trailer for this long, she had been sure Star would dance around at least a little.

"I hate to say it, but we might have to find a bighorn sheep to nudge that horse in the butt if he doesn't start showing a little more spunk," Cal said, taking off his cowboy hat and scratching his head.

Christina's shoulders slumped, but she was too tired and discouraged even to get annoyed at the thoughtless comment.

After they loaded up the horses once more and bought sodas from a vending machine, they set out on their way again. This time Cal was driving. Settling into her seat, Gwen cracked open her soda and tapped her can against Christina's.

"Don't let your worries get the best of you," she said.

Christina nodded wearily. "I just don't understand it. I thought everything would be all right after Star recovered. I figured the only thing I had to worry about was getting him into condition. But Star's totally changed. It's like I don't even know him anymore."

"Lyssa says he was pretty sick. It might have been a little much to expect him to spring right back," Gwen said.

"I didn't think he'd spring back overnight, but I never dreamed that he'd start acting like he didn't even know me," Christina replied.

"I had a burro like that once," Cal began, but Gwen shot him a look.

"Horses and burros aren't the same," she said.

Cal drummed his fingers on the steering wheel. "Well, I think you're doing the right thing, bringing him out to Lyssa. If anyone can sort him out, that girl can."

"She has a touch, that girl," Gwen added with a nod.

"Yeah, I think she's great, too," Christina said. Silently she added, *I just hope she can help Star.*

Closing her eyes wearily, she pictured Star in the old days, bursting with power and fire. Oh, she'd give anything to see him like that again!

5

THE LONGER THEY TRAVELED, THE MORE CHRISTINA BECAME aware of her surroundings. The rolling hills and farmland were giving way to a starker landscape, punctuated by low brush and rocky areas. After they had made their way over a mountain range, Christina took note of how harsh and wild the land was becoming. With fewer and fewer natural obstacles to break up the view, she found her eyes could sweep for miles until they hit the horizon. It was always something she'd noticed about Lyssa, the way her eyes seemed to take in miles at a glance. And now she knew why.

"We're in Montana now. It's beautiful out here, isn't it?" Gwen said, following her gaze. "We're just northeast of Yellowstone."

Christina nodded, but she shivered and fought the

impulse to burrow into the warmth of her fleece pullover.

"Well, after what you're used to, it might take a while for you to warm to our part of the country," Cal admitted. "Won't be long now."

He reached for a squashed pack of gum and held out a piece for Christina.

Christina took it and chewed, trying to smile bravely. It didn't matter what Montana looked like, she told herself. If Lyssa could help bring back the old Star, that was the only thing that counted.

That evening the sun set in a dazzling display of orange. Hypnotized by the white lines and oncoming headlights, Christina dozed again. Suddenly she felt Gwen nudging her. She pointed, and Christina's eyes traveled to the simple wooden sign that formed part of the arch over the dirt road. In the light from the headlights, she read the name: Thunder Ranch. They had arrived!

"But I thought it was called the *Black* Thunder Ranch," Christina said.

"Well, the ranch records show it officially as Thunder Ranch. Black Thunder is just a nickname. That's because a few years ago coal deposits were discovered in the northern pastures. Lyssa's dad was offered a lot of money to let it be mined, but he didn't want to scar up the land," Cal explained as Gwen scrambled out to open the rusted metal double gates that were across the dirt road.

Bouncing along the rain-rutted road, Christina glanced into the side mirrors. She prayed Star wasn't being jostled too much. In the dim beams thrown off by the truck, she could see barbed wire fences running along both sides of the road. She gulped. *Is there going to be room in the barn for Star?* No way was she putting her horse in any field surrounded by barbed wire, she thought frantically.

"How big is it?" she asked, trying to make conversation to settle her nerves.

"All told, the ranch is a few thousand acres," Cal said as they rumbled across a cattle guard that crossed over a rushing creek.

Just then Christina caught sight of a familiar flea-bitten gray horse headed toward them. They drew closer, and Christina's face broke into a grin as Lyssa came into view. She was wearing a Navajo wool poncho and worn leather chaps. She took off her black cowboy hat and waved it, revealing her long black hair hanging loosely past her shoulders. She whooped loudly and peered down at them, grinning from ear to ear, as the truck pulled up alongside her.

"Lyssa Hynde, you know better than to be out here in the dark," Gwen called out the window.

Lyssa rode around to Christina's side and reached

down to squeeze her hand in welcome. "Blue's not afraid of the dark. Anyway, I had to come out here and meet you all."

"Well, you shouldn't be whooping so loudly. You know everyone's probably bunked down for the night," Gwen huffed. She turned to Christina. "Morning comes early around here," she explained.

Lyssa winked at Christina. "Oh, Aunt Gwen, everyone's still up. They're all in the great room waiting to meet you and Christina. I've been filling their heads with stories all night."

With that, she turned Blue. "Meet you at the barn," she called over her shoulder. "I've got Star's box stall all spruced up."

Christina suppressed a loud sigh of relief.

Minutes later they'd pulled up in front of a large wooden barn that was lit outside by a floodlight. Cal opened the tailgate, and Christina snapped Star's lead shank on, backing him slowly and carefully down the ramp. Her eyes scoured him carefully, but he appeared to have traveled well. She ran her hands up and down his legs.

"All this way and no swelling," she said happily.

"Which is more than I can say for this guy," said Cal, frowning as he felt the gray pony's hock.

Lyssa knelt down by the pony for a closer look. "Not too bad," she said. "We'll get that swelling taken care of. The kids here will be excited to see this little guy. Hmmm. Now I have to think of a name for him." Then she turned to Christina and gave her a hug. "I'm so glad you came."

"Thanks for having us," Christina said. "I know how busy your family is with your new group of guests."

Lyssa rolled her eyes. "A seriously wimpy batch," she whispered. "But there are a few horse-crazy kids, and they're lots of fun. Let me help Aunt Gwen with these heifers, and then let's get Star settled in for the night."

As they walked into the lighted interior of the oversized barn, Christina could see it was airy and new. Oddly, though, there was a large tractor just inside the door that seemed to serve as a tack rack. Ropes and bridles were draped over the hood, and there were large Western saddles perched on each wheel.

"As I told you before, we've got a ton of work to do here," Lyssa explained, following Christina's gaze. "We've been so busy with our guests, we haven't had time to replace the tractor shed that blew down in the ice storm last winter."

"At least your daddy and Cal were able to complete the new barn in time for that storm," Gwen said, leading in the pony and tossing the heifers' ropes on top of the towering stack on the tractor.

Lyssa laughed. "That's true. That old barn had

been around for a hundred years. We were sure that one day it would just give up and fall down."

"Put the pony back by the puppies," she said to her aunt, then turned to Christina. "Our Australian shepherd had puppies a few weeks ago. They're so cute. I'll show them to you tomorrow.

"We'll put Star here," she went on, pointing to a roomy stall filled with fresh bedding. She jerked her thumb toward a small barred window across from it. "Our foreman's son, Mitch, has night watch, and he promised to keep an eye on Star for you."

Christina nodded gratefully as she brought Star into the stall. Yawning and stumbling in the thick bedding, she suddenly realized how tired she was.

Lyssa grinned at her. "Let's get this big guy settled. Then we can say hello to everyone. My mom and dad are dying to meet you. I've been telling them all about you and Star."

"I can't wait to meet them," said Christina, although she didn't want to leave Star. After all, it was a strange, new place for him.

"We're pretty full right now, but I got you your own bunk right next to the ladies' bunk. It's downstairs, right below the kitchen," Lyssa said.

"Actually," said Christina, turning around to face Lyssa, "if you don't mind, I'd like to bed down here with Star."

Lyssa nodded. "I don't blame you, but honestly, the house is just up that path. And Mitch is the best. If Star even wiggles his ears wrong, I promise you he'll come get you know in a flash."

"I don't know . . ." Christina's voice trailed away as she fussed over Star's blanket, checked his water bucket, and fluffed up his bedding.

Lyssa touched her arm. "Come on. You can check on him before you turn in."

Nodding reluctantly, Christina let herself out of Star's stall.

Lyssa peered at her more closely. "You okay? You looked totally wiped."

"Yeah, I am a little beat. I think it's all the worrying over Star these past few weeks," Christina admitted as she latched the stall door.

"Well, you've come to the right place. We'll get inside that horse's head and get you two back on track in no time," Lyssa said.

Christina followed Lyssa out into the corral, where Cal was unhitching the trailer by flashlight.

"Night, girls," he called.

"Thank you again for bringing us here," Christina called back.

Cal waved, and Lyssa pointed to the brightly lit house. "See?" Lyssa was saying. "I told you the main house is really close. The men's bunkhouse is over to the right of the house. The feed barn and the wagon barn are just down that road. That's next to the practice track we graded a couple of years ago. My dressage arena is just up there," she exclaimed, pointing in another direction.

Christina peered into the inky blackness. "I have to tell you, I can't see a thing," she said.

"Uh, right. Well, I'll show you everything in the morning," Lyssa said. "Let's go up to the house."

Leading the way, Lyssa started up the path. Twice Christina slipped on icy patches of snow. Winter had already hit Montana.

The house was warm and inviting. Christina felt instantly at home as she took in the vast great room crowded with people of all ages, who were gathered around a stone fireplace laughing and playing board games.

"These are my parents," said Lyssa, smiling proudly. "Marcy and Rob Hynde."

Christina shook hands with both of them.

"Welcome," said her mother, who was an older version of Lyssa, with black hair and sparkling blue eyes.

Mr. Hynde's face was deeply tanned, and he was wearing worn jeans with a large silver trophy buckle. Christina had particularly wanted to meet him after hearing the stories of his injuries from falling off a wild horse and his long road to recovery. Parker had told her about how the family had almost lost the ranch, and how Lyssa and her aunt, uncle, and mom had converted it into a dude ranch to turn their luck around. From Gwen's stories Christina knew that the ranch wasn't totally out of the woods yet, but things were looking up. Looking at Lyssa's mom and dad, Christina couldn't see any signs of their troubles, only a genuine warmth and friendliness.

Lyssa turned and with a sweeping gesture introduced Christina to the roomful of people. "Everybody, meet Christina Reese," she said.

Christina found herself looking into the faces of several adults and a few children, including two girls who looked exactly alike. They seemed to be about eleven years old.

"That's Caitlin and Cameron. They're twins," Lyssa explained. Her voice dropped to a whisper. "You'll love them. They're so sweet."

Going around the room, Lyssa introduced the other guests. "These are their parents, Jim and Grace Hale. These two guys are Brad and Jeremy. Brad's thirteen, and Jeremy's twelve." she said, motioning to two boys who were playing a board game with two middle-aged women. "That's their aunt, Mrs. Talbot, and her sister Ms. Macintyre, from Canada. Ty and Sara Fuller, their cousin, Grant. They're from Florida. This is Casey, Brenna, and Jacqueline. They're all roommates from the University of Virginia. This is Henrik. He's from Denmark. And this is Ray," Lyssa added.

Christina smiled at everyone, wondering how she'd ever remember all the names. Then she glanced at Ray, who looked to be about her age. He was wearing tight new jeans and shiny snakeskin boots with high heels. Instantly Christina recognized him as one of the city slickers Lyssa had been referring to.

"You the one with the horse whose spirit's broken?" the guy said, coolly looking Christina over.

Christina felt an angry retort rise to her lips, but she bit it back. There was no need to start off on the wrong foot with people she'd never met before.

Mr. Hynde stepped in. "A setback, that's all," he said in a polite but firm tone. "Nothing that can't be fixed."

"I read somewhere that once a horse's spirit is broken, you can't ever get it back again," Ray pressed on. He turned to follow some of the other male guests, who were starting toward the side door to head for their bunks for the night.

"Not true," Lyssa said decisively. "Anyway, Star's spirit isn't broken. Good night, everyone." She took Christina's arm. "Come on, I'll show you to your bunk."

Christina followed her down a flight of narrow stairs.

71

"Ignore that creep," Lyssa said in a low voice. "Ray comes from Arizona, and he'd never been on a horse in his life before he came here. A couple of days in the saddle on old Gepetto—that's the horse we always put the absolute beginners on—and he thinks he's an expert. He also thinks the girls are crazy for him, but that's another story."

Christina giggled and shook her head.

"Ta-da," Lyssa exclaimed, turning on the light in a small but comfortable-looking room. "Here you go. I hope you like it."

"Oh, it's great. Thanks," Christina said, looking around. The walls were painted beige, and there were twig-framed pictures of horses on the range. The bed was covered with a brightly colored Navajo blanket, and there was an upholstered chair next to a small table with a laptop computer on it.

"I put my computer in here in case you need it for your schoolwork," Lyssa said.

"Thanks, but I brought my own," Christina said, setting down her bag and thinking guiltily of the two assignments that were already late. She could E-mail them in the morning, she decided.

"The women's rooms are across the hall, and the bathroom is down the hallway to your right. We start early around here, but feel free to sleep in if you want to catch up. Well, good night."

Christina nodded as Lyssa left the room. *As if I could sleep,* she thought. She sat on the bed, taking in her surroundings. Looking out the window, she caught sight of a shooting star. She had never seen so many stars in her life.

Taking a deep breath, she tried to swallow her uneasy feelings. Okay, so she was in a strange place. But it was Star's best hope. She was just going to have to roll with everything and make it work. Laying her head on the pillow, she looked up at the ceiling.

"Please let Star be okay," she said aloud. Then she realized she hadn't looked in on him again. She was just so tired.

At that moment Christina heard a lone coyote's howl somewhere off in the distance, and her eyes flew open.

That's it, Christina decided. *There's no way I can leave Star alone in some strange barn out here in the middle of nowhere!*

But then her eyelids drooped, and before she knew it she was sound asleep.

6

"DON'T WORRY, SWEETIE, I'M STILL HERE," CHRISTINA CALLED early the next morning as she stumbled down the path to the barn in the darkness.

She knew she was being silly, but she couldn't help feeling relieved that a coyote hadn't sneaked into the barn during the night. The next minute she almost jumped out of her skin as she heard the sound of frantic claws against Star's stall door, followed by a series of tiny barks.

Oh, it must be the puppies Lyssa told me about. Stop being such a wimp, Christina told herself sternly.

"Good thing we brought an extra blanket for you," she murmured, her teeth chattering as she adjusted the surcingles of Star's thick blanket. "It's cold here, huh, big guy?"

In the semidarkness Christina could see Star regarding her, but otherwise he didn't respond as she fussed over him. He didn't even turn his head when one of the puppies nosed its way through the half-open door.

"Out with you," Christina said, pushing the wriggling gray form back through the door. "I'll come play with you in a while, but I don't want you to get trampled."

Stepping out and closing the door behind her, she went over to an opened bale of hay that Cal had unloaded the night before, and pulled off a flake. "Look," she said, returning to Star's stall. "I brought you a yummy breakfast."

She dumped the hay in the manger and pulled a carrot out of her pocket. Star took it gently from her fingers and crunched calmly before pushing his face into his hay.

Well, at least the trip didn't put him off his feed, Christina thought, watching him munch for a few moments.

Then curiosity about her new surroundings got the better of her. Moving to the stall window, Christina gazed out. She could hear cattle mooing off in the distance, but she couldn't see any. In the half-light she could just make out the corral, fenced by rough-hewn logs. Beyond that, she could see a light on in the main part of the house that she knew to be the kitchen. Probably Mrs. Hynde was already up to prepare a mountain of food for the ranch guests.

Christina could picture Lyssa's mother cooking next to the big room where she'd met all the guests the night before. Christina hadn't paid much attention to the room then, but she hadn't been able to miss the way Lyssa's family's love of horses was displayed everywhere. The pine-paneled walls were covered with old photos of horses, and ribbons from horse shows hung on baling wire stretched over the stone fireplace. There was a silver-covered trophy saddle slung over the back of a chair, and trophy bowls and cups were jammed into the china cabinet. Christina decided that later, when she had time, she'd have to get a closer look at those pictures.

"Well, you're up, but why aren't you saddled up?"

Christina turned around. To her surprise, there was Lyssa outside the stall door mounted on a short, stocky buckskin. As Christina made her way over to the door, she could see that Lyssa was riding with a loop of wire around the horse's neck, but no saddle or bridle. Lyssa's long, blue-jean-clad legs dangled well below the buckskin's belly, and her worn moccasins were absurdly near the ground. She smiled as she remembered how annoyed Parker had been that Lyssa had ridden without any tack, calling it an attention-getting gimmick.

"Do you ever give your poor horses a rest?" Christina joked. "Riding late at night, and now again before it's even dawn?"

Lyssa grinned lopsidedly. "Oh, I wouldn't call it a *ride*. This old love bucket just helped me bring down some of the horses from the hill pasture over there for the guests. B.C. just sleepwalked his way down the hill, and now he gets breakfast in bed."

She slid off and slipped the loop of wire over B.C.'s head, then patted him on his hindquarters. The buckskin shuffled off down the barn aisle. Christina watched in amazement as he opened the latch on a nearby stall door and nosed his way in.

Lyssa grabbed an armful of hay and tossed it in the buckskin's stall, leaving the door open as she stepped out.

"Do you let all your horses cruise around totally free?" Christina asked.

Lyssa shook her head. "Nope. Only Blue and this guy here. Oh, and Lady, of course. They have special privileges—the run of the ranch, you might say. Of course, my mom gets mad when Blue comes into the kitchen."

Christina raised her eyebrows. "In the kitchen?" she repeated.

But Lyssa's attention was now on Star. She gave him a long, appraising look.

"From what you told me, I expected him to look worse," she said honestly. "His coat doesn't look bad, and he isn't as thin as I thought he'd be."

Christina turned to Star. "Well, you should have seen him before. His coat isn't as glossy as it was, but it's come a long way. I've been grooming him like crazy and massaging him and everything. And look at him wolf down his breakfast," she added happily.

Lyssa nodded. "I think he knows he needs to get his strength back. Some horses just know what's good for them."

Christina's face clouded. "Yeah," she said quietly.

Lyssa's face split into a big grin. "Well, anyway, it's great to see you again, and I have a good feeling that we'll get your Star back on his feet. Now let's go get some chow, and you can tell me what everyone's up to."

Christina stepped over the patches of snow and pushed her way past a throng of multicolored horses eating from long mangers in the corral just outside the barn. Three or four of them converged on Lyssa, jealously squealing at each other and nosing her pockets for treats.

"These are the horses old B.C. and I just brought in," Lyssa said, laughing as she tried to shoo them off. "Go on," she scolded the horses, looking them in the eye. "Go eat your breakfast."

"How many horses do you have?" Christina asked as she followed Lyssa to the house.

Lyssa tossed her thick black braid over her shoulder as she wrinkled her nose and counted silently, moving her lips. "I'd say about fifty. But they're not all suitable for our guests. Sometimes the Johnsons next door lend us a few well-broke horses when we have more guests than we counted on."

"And how many guests do you have at a time?" Christina asked.

"Oh, usually not more than fifteen or sixteen. What you saw last night was about the maximum. We like to give everyone lots of personal attention so they can feel right at home instead of like they're on an assembly line. We get a few kids and families, but mostly we tend to draw the business types who want time out from job stress."

Christina watched several of the guests coming toward them from the men's bunkhouse. She could easily picture all of them in suits and ties instead of the new cowboy outfits they had obviously bought just for the trip.

They waved when they saw Lyssa, and turned up the path to the kitchen door. Christina saw that Ray was hanging back behind the others, obviously not quite part of the chattering, laughing group. His eyes fixed on her suddenly, and Christina looked away.

"Mitch is going to take everyone on a trail ride this morning after breakfast," Lyssa said. "Just over that hill by the Johnsons' spread, you get a really good view of the Beartooth Mountains."

Christina lifted her eyes to where Lyssa was pointing. Off in the distance she could see the mountains, now partially obscured by a stand of scraggly trees.

"That's where the summer pasture is. I've got a couple more horses I've got to bring down the mountain sometime next week. The weather will start taking a turn pretty soon, and I don't want the old guys to get stuck up there."

Lyssa turned in the other direction. "The river's over there. Maybe you and I'll go take a look at it later."

"Sounds good," said Christina agreeably.

When she and Lyssa entered the kitchen, they were greeted by the smells of a traditional ranch breakfast. The long trestle table was already filled with guests, but Mr. Hynde patted an empty seat in between him and Gwen. "Christina, load up your plate and then sit right here," he called.

Christina made her way down the buffet line, scooping up a mound of scrambled eggs mixed with onions, peppers, and cheese. Breathing deeply, she inhaled the scent of frying bacon. She helped herself to a couple of pieces and felt her mouth water. The next minute she blinked in surprise as Mrs. Hynde poured a spoonful of salsa over her eggs.

"Go ahead and try it, you'll like it," said Ray, coming up behind her in the line.

Christina smiled gamely. "I'm sure I will," she said with forced politeness. She didn't think she'd like sauce over her eggs, but she didn't want to give Ray anything to talk to her about. She got the creepy feeling that he had made a point of standing next to her in the buffet line. Taking a biscuit and a cup of hot chocolate, she made her way over to the table and sat down, relieved to be flanked by Lyssa's family so that Ray couldn't sit next to her.

Mr. Hynde introduced her again to Henrik, the gray-haired banker from Denmark who spoke flawless English, then to the young family with the twin girls. "You met the Hales. They're from San Francisco. And you met these horse-crazy twins, Caitlin and Cameron."

"Horse-crazy, huh? I have a feeling we'll get along really well," Christina said, smiling at the girls. They were wearing identical red-checked shirts and they had the same solemn green eyes and thick red hair.

Gwen leaned over the table and gestured with her fork. "Hey, girls, did you know Christina is a real live jockey?"

"Wow," said Caitlin, staring at Christina.

"An apprentice, actually," Christina admitted.

"You ride real racehorses?" asked Cameron.

Lyssa called across the table, "You bet. And she even brought her racehorse here to visit us at the Black Thunder."

"That the horse whose spirit is broken?" chimed in Ray.

Cal cleared his throat loudly before Christina could say anything, and started in on the morning announcements. Christina half listened to the talk of trail rides and roping lessons while she gazed out the windows at the ranch spread out below. She knew better than to listen to Ray, but she couldn't help worrying over Star once more.

She ate quickly, anxious to get out and ride, and then she and Lyssa returned to the barn.

"Uncle Cal's filling in for me this morning. Normally I'd be out there matching saddles to horses and riders and trying to keep people from getting stepped on or worse," Lyssa said, jerking her chin toward the corral area, where Christina could hear voices ringing and hooves stamping.

"Look out!" she heard Cal shout.

Christina smiled. "It sounds like fun," she said.

"It is, but it can be a real pain when so many people need help at once," Lyssa said. She shook her head. "Well, no point in jawing all day. Let's saddle up and I'll give you a tour."

Christina smiled. "I'd like that. I've heard so much about this place. It'll be so cool to see it at last. But I don't think I'll ride today. It's probably better to hand-walk Star till he gets used to things."

Lyssa nodded. "Yeah, I guess you're right."

A few moments later Christina led Star out of the barn and into the corral, where Cal and some of the hands were helping guests saddle up for their day's activities.

"Hey, Lyssa, you loafer. Taking the day off?" teased Mitch, who had just given a leg up to one of the younger kids. He was powerfully built, with a black hat that partially covered his wavy brown hair. His grin showed a row of perfectly even teeth.

Lyssa nodded. "Yep. I'm going to show my friend and her horse around. Her name's Christina, and she's from Kentucky."

The guy glanced at Christina and then his eyes traveled to Star, who was standing in the dazzling sunrise, the sun glinting off his chestnut coat and highlighting the shadows of his ribs. Mitch took off his black hat in a gesture of introduction. "You need to get some meat on that fancy horse's bones."

"Mind your own business," replied Lyssa good-naturedly. She turned to Christina. "He has an opinion on everything, but he's got a heart of gold."

Seeing the look on Christina's face, she turned and

yelled playfully at Mitch, "You'd better take it back, Mitch, or she'll challenge you to a race. Star's way fast!"

Christina had only been at the ranch for a few hours, and already several strangers had opinions on Star. People around here sure had no trouble telling a person what they thought! It took a little getting used to.

Lyssa lifted the loop of baling wire that held the gate and swung it open so that Christina and Star could pass through. Stopping at the rise just beyond the corral, Lyssa shielded her eyes against the sun, turning around and watching as the guests mounted up.

"I would have loved coming here when I was a kid," Christina said. "All these horses! It's right out of one of those old movies."

Lyssa smiled. "You mean you didn't get enough where you grew up?"

Christina laughed. "There are never enough horses."

Christina looked politely at the cattle, then said, "Tell me more about the horses. I'll bet you have your work cut out finding horses that are safe for beginners to ride but that can still get the ranch work done."

Nodding, Lyssa said, "We got lucky. A few months back, my dad, Uncle Cal, and I got some really nice mustangs at one of the roundups, and we gentled them all. There are one or two I don't let the beginners ride, but most of them are bombproof."

She pointed to a flattened area, where Christina

could see that several jumps had been set up. "Of course, it's not all mustangs and roundups these days. Blue and I have a pretty rigorous training schedule. That's where I do my stadium work, and over there, behind that clump of trees, is where the cross-country course is," Lyssa said.

Christina gazed at the freshly painted red-and-white jumps. They looked so out of place among the barbed wire fences and cattle. It still amazed her that Lyssa was training for the Olympics, just as Parker was—and helping her family run the dude ranch at the same time. "You have a pretty intense schedule. Do you ever sleep?" she joked.

Lyssa's blue eyes sparkled. "There'll be time to rest when I win that Olympic medal," she said.

Christina was tempted to add, *And I'll rest after Star and I win the Derby,* but as she turned to look at Star, her voice caught in her throat. He was looking more and more like his old self physically, but Christina could see that the light in his eyes still wasn't quite there.

Seeing Christina's expression, Lyssa rested her hand on her shoulder. "I have one order for you while you're here at the Black Thunder. I know that Star will come around. So no more fretting, got it?"

I wish it were that easy, thought Christina, but she smiled thinly and nodded.

"Now come on. I've got lots more to show you."

They had just turned toward the creek when Star whirled around, pulling the rope right out of Christina's hands. Christina immediately leaped to catch the rope, but Star jumped away and trotted down along the creek bank.

"I can't believe he did that," Christina exclaimed.

Lyssa held up her hand as Christina started off after Star. "Wait, Christina. Let him go," she said.

"Let him go? Are you kidding?" she exclaimed.

"He can't really go anywhere," Lyssa said. "Right past where it turns, there's a fence. He probably won't jump into the creek, and there's a shed on the other side. He doesn't have a way out."

"But he might step on the lead and hurt himself," Christina protested.

"Just don't chase him," Lyssa said gently. "He might be a little slow these days, but he can still outrun you—and that's what he'll do if you chase him. Let him come to you."

Christina opened her mouth and then shut it. It was confusing. On one hand, she'd come here for Lyssa's advice, but on the other hand, what the other girl was suggesting was just too dangerous. She had visions of Star galloping across the open country, running for miles before stepping in a rabbit hole or getting caught in barbed wire or breaking a leg on the tangled lead.

"Star's challenging your leadership," Lyssa said,

looking thoughtfully at Star's disappearing hindquarters. "Let's just walk along here slowly, and when we catch up to him, we'll just stand there. You've got to make eye contact and establish yourself as the alpha leader. Then you'll make him submit and come to you."

Christina bit her lip. "Alpha leader?" she asked dubiously.

Lyssa nodded her head. "It goes back for thousands of years. When horses ran in wild bands, there was always a leader. You can't boss a horse around, but you do have to be that alpha leader, or you and your horse won't ever agree on anything."

"I see," Christina said. Privately she thought it sounded a little over the top, but she wasn't in any position to argue. "Fine." But she quickened her pace, eager to catch up to Star.

Lyssa pointed out the practice racetrack that was up on the ridge on the other side of the creek. But Christina only half listened to her, her focus on Star.

When they rounded the curve of the creek, Christina saw Star ahead, his nose in the brown grass. Just as Lyssa had said, Star had stopped at the fence, boxed in by a shed on one side and the creek on the other. He lifted his head at their approach, neck arched and nostrils flaring. Christina was amazed by how beautiful and wild he looked, poised to run.

"Walk slowly toward him, and don't let your eyes

move from his for a moment," Lyssa said in a calm voice. "Talk to him. Reassure him. Reestablish the connection."

Nervously Christina walked toward Star the way Lyssa had instructed, her eyes locked onto his. "Come on, sweetie," she said steadily. "Nothing's going to hurt you."

Star stood perfectly still and allowed her to catch him.

Lyssa stood back, watching as Christina led Star toward her. "That was a big step," she said.

"Uh, yeah," Christina said. She was relieved that Star was unhurt. But it wasn't as though anything had really been resolved. Star had gotten spooked by something and then, like always, he'd allowed her to catch him.

"Let's go up to this rise over here," Lyssa said. "There's a really good view of the mountains, and we can watch the guests come up the trail."

A few minutes later she and Lyssa came to a large flat rock.

"Okay, Chris," said Lyssa, her blue eyes looking straight into Christina's. "Now lead Star up onto the rock."

"I'll try, but Star's not going to the edge," mumbled Christina, moving gingerly onto the rock. Satisfied that the footing was okay, she urged Star forward. Star hesitated but then stepped onto the rock. They walked a couple of feet until Lyssa held up her hand, then dropped to her stomach and wiggled like a snake a few inches to the edge.

Christina let out Star's lead rope as far as she could without pulling Star any closer to the edge. Below, the valley spread out at their feet. Christina saw miles and miles of wavy brown grass, broken up every so often by a few trees and rock piles.

"It's beautiful," she gasped.

"You should really bring Star closer so you can see better," Lyssa exclaimed.

Christina shook her head as they heard hoofbeats coming up the trail below them. Star lifted his head, nostrils flaring and muscles quivering at the sound of the approaching horses.

Christina gulped, afraid to move. What if Star bolted and fell off the rock? He'd plunge to his death! Why had she allowed herself to do such a stupid thing, anyway?

Lyssa didn't turn to look at Christina. Her eyes were intent on the horses and riders. "Ease that choke hold on Star's rope," she said quietly. "He's got to trust you." Christina stood frozen as the riders went past underneath them, ready to leap in front of Star if he moved. But he merely stood there, filling his nostrils with the horses' scent.

"Good," Lyssa said, backing up. Then she stood and walked back to the trail.

"That's it?" Christina asked as she led Star off the rock behind Lyssa.

"Just part of the process," Lyssa said. "Baby steps. Each time you and Star are put into situations where you have to trust each other, you strengthen the bond. If you're looking for big drama, you probably won't find it."

Rolling her eyes as she followed Lyssa, Christina wondered for the hundredth time if she'd temporarily lost her mind when she decided to bring Star there. She'd only been there for part of a day, and already she'd risked Star's life not once but twice!

7

THAT EVENING AFTER SUPPER CHRISTINA BEDDED STAR down and allowed Lyssa to persuade her to come up to the great room, where several of the guests were hanging around after a long day playing on the ranch.

"Just relax with everyone and have a good time," Lyssa said. "You need a break from worrying about Star all the time. You'll help him a lot more if you have a fresh perspective."

Christina enjoyed the good-natured banter and playing a board game called Corral that Horse! with the twins. She even managed to sidestep Ray, who seemed to be everywhere she turned. But she couldn't stop yawning, and after checking on Star she went back to her bunk and fell asleep soon after her head touched the pillow.

The next day at breakfast the guests were buzzing about a trip to Billings, where they were going to buy more comfortable boots and clothing.

"I need a hat like Lyssa's," said Caitlin, looking enviously at Lyssa's rumpled teal hat, which was hanging from a hook by its stampede string. "My hat falls off the minute my horse trots."

"You don't need a new hat," Mrs. Hynde exclaimed, pouring coffee. "Lyssa will tie a stampede string on for you so your hat stays put. It's just a strip of rawhide."

"Well, I need a good pair of boots. These are killing me," complained the banker from Denmark, holding up a pair of shiny snakeskin cowboy boots.

Lyssa leaned over to whisper to Christina, "That always happens. They arrive with their suitcases crammed with things that are all the rage in Los Angeles or Chicago, and then find out that they're the pits out on the range." She looked meaningfully at Ray's too-tight jeans. "How he can ride in those things, I'll never know."

Christina giggled and sipped her hot chocolate, trying not to look. She didn't want to give Ray an opening to chime in with more of his stupid comments about Star. She had enough worries of her own when it came to her horse.

When Mrs. Hynde asked her if she wanted to join everyone on their shopping trip, Christina shook her head. It might have been fun, but every day on the ranch with Star was precious. She wanted to hand-walk him again that day and get him more used to the new sights and sounds. Then she wanted to ride him and try whatever else Lyssa suggested—as long as it wasn't too dangerous.

After the guests took off for Billings, Lyssa and Christina helped Mrs. Hynde in the kitchen, then hurried down to the barn.

Christina led Star out of his stall and hitched him to an eyebolt in the wall by the tractor. She still couldn't get used to the idea that there weren't any crossties around. Lyssa gave a shrill whistle, and Blue came ambling into the barn unassisted, the puppies and their mother darting around near his feet.

Standing seventeen hands, Blue was a huge horse with oversized ears and hooves to match. He'd muscled up in the months since Christina had seen him last, and he looked fit and ready for anything.

"He looks great," she said, picking up a brush and starting to groom Star.

Lyssa patted the gray's neck proudly. "Thanks," she said. "We've been doing all kinds of fitness gallops to increase his stamina and build those muscles. It's paying off, I think."

Just then one of the puppies raced right between Star's legs, yipping excitedly. Christina rushed to

Star's head to quiet him, but Star didn't even flinch.

"I don't get it," Christina said, dumbfounded. "Star used to be so sensitive. I'm beginning to think he's undergone a total personality change."

Lyssa studied Star for a moment. "I don't think it's a personality change. It's more like what you said to me on the phone—that you two have stopped talking. He just needs to reconnect with you. That's what we were starting to do yesterday."

Christina scrunched her nose as she wiped Star's face with a towel. She wasn't so sure that anything had been accomplished yesterday. She had already been gone from home for four days, and she could only stay a few more days before she'd have to head home again. Surely there was more she could do that didn't involve scaling rocks.

Lyssa cleaned out Blue's hooves with a pick, then straightened up. "Now tell me where you put your saddle, and I'll go get it for you."

"Oh, that's okay," said Christina casually, "I won't be needing my saddle. I think I'll just hand-walk Star again today. He needs another day to get acclimated."

Lyssa shrugged. "He seems acclimated to me—cattle, tractors, puppies. It won't make a difference if you're on his back."

Christina considered her words for a moment. She didn't want to admit it, but she was afraid that even in

94

his strange, new surroundings, Star would keep up his odd behavior. "It was an awfully long haul out here. Don't you think it's kind of soon?"

Looking up, she found herself in a lock with Lyssa's blue eyes. After a couple of seconds Christina looked away.

"Oh, all right," she said reluctantly.

"Cool," said Lyssa. "Now where's that saddle?"

As Christina finished grooming, she scowled. *How does Lyssa always manage to get her way?* she wondered.

A few moments later she was mounted and heading out through the main corral. Lyssa rode toward her on Blue, saddleless and bridleless, as usual.

Lyssa smiled. "Let's go!"

Christina's heart lifted as she felt some of Lyssa's enthusiasm rub off on her. "Move 'em out, big guy," she said loudly, picking up her reins and urging Star forward.

"I'd be a little careful here," Lyssa called back as she started over the cattle guard. "Horses that haven't been on one of these things tend to freak when they're ridden over them."

Star walked right across quietly, and Christina patted his neck. "Good boy," she said.

Christina concentrated on trying to read Star's body language as they made their way across an open field. Star didn't seem interested in his new surroundings at all. His ears flopped along as he walked, and while he wasn't exactly resisting, he didn't have any of his old fire, either. She nudged him every so often in an attempt to keep his walk at a steady pace. Soon her legs were tired and she felt her frustration mounting.

After a few minutes Lyssa twisted in her saddle and looked back. "Are you ready to trot?" she asked.

"Sure," Christina called. She was conscious that although they'd only been walking a short while, Star had fallen well behind Blue.

Blue started off at a brisk trot over the brown grass, and Christina cued Star to follow. To her dismay, Star ignored her. She nudged him forward again as Blue and Lyssa disappeared around a sizable boulder.

When Star finally picked up a trot, Christina took him around the boulder, just in time to see Lyssa up ahead, lifting a loop of baling wire that secured the pasture gate.

"This is the lower pasture—it'll bring us down by the reservoir. We can get the horses a drink," Lyssa shouted back to her.

Christina nodded wearily. Watching as Blue nosed open the gate on command, she couldn't help feeling envious. Blue seemed to read Lyssa's mind.

Closing the gate behind them, Lyssa led the way along the fence line. They walked along for a few minutes in silence. Instead of letting her envy get the better of her, Christina tried to distract herself by looking at the rugged, barren landscape, so different from the lush, rolling fields of Kentucky.

You could ride for miles and not bump into a living thing, she marveled.

That is, she reminded herself a few minutes later, *except for cattle.* As they approached the rise, Christina could see what looked like hundreds of cows dotting the huge pasture in front of them.

"Those are steers," Lyssa said. "We'll be working them over the next couple of weeks, worming and vaccinating."

Lyssa turned Blue abruptly to the right and shot off into a canter. "I'll show you our new Angus bull. We bought him at the fair a couple of months ago," she yelled, her voice trailing off.

But Christina wasn't listening. She leaned forward, instinctively preparing for Star to react to Blue's sudden movement. After all, generations of breeding had programmed him to overtake any horse in front of him. But Star merely walked on and paid no attention to the thundering hooves ahead of him.

"Well, we shouldn't be galloping across unfamiliar ground anyway," Christina muttered to herself. "There could be rabbit holes or—or rocks, or something."

Still, it was maddening to choke in the thick dust in Blue's wake and know there was nothing she could do.

She kicked Star into a poky trot, and when they caught up to Blue, Lyssa raised her eyebrows. "A little slow on the draw, huh?" she observed.

Christina blew out her breath. "I told you he wasn't ready. I think all this open land is rattling him."

Lyssa looked meaningfully at Star. "He doesn't look rattled."

"Well, now you know what I've been talking about," Christina said, setting her reins on Star's neck.

"He doesn't look depressed, though," Lyssa added.

"How can you tell?"

"His body language. I think there's another problem."

Christina was mystified. "What?"

But Lyssa merely touched the wire loop around Blue's neck and rode off a few feet, pointing to a large black bull that was scratching his back on a wooden post in the middle of the bull pasture next to them.

"That's our guy," Lyssa said. "We call him Webster. My cousin Travis named him. Isn't his conformation amazing?"

Christina nodded, though she had no idea what exactly qualified as good conformation in a bull. She was about to ask Lyssa whether Webster was mean when suddenly Star whirled, nearly throwing her to the ground. Christina clutched his mane and hung on for dear life.

"Whoa, I didn't see that coming," Lyssa exclaimed.

Christina sat back and regained her seat. "Easy now, Star," she murmured.

Star tossed his head and tucked his quarters under him, ready to whirl again.

"Let him take a look," Lyssa suggested. "Turn him toward Webster."

Christina opened her right rein slightly and shifted her weight. Star turned quickly, but he didn't seem to want to look at the bull. His ears flicked back, signaling that his interest was elsewhere.

"That's weird. I don't think he's worried about the bull at all," Lyssa said slowly, shaking her head.

"I don't, either," Christina said. "But I wish I knew what he was worried about."

"Hate to say it, but I think he's just decided not to work with you," Lyssa said.

"That's for sure," grumbled Christina.

"Come on, let's go over to the reservoir," Lyssa exclaimed. "I have an idea."

"Good, because I'm totally out of ideas," Christina said crossly.

They started off again. Star walked resentfully, every so often stopping and backing up a few steps. Soon he was far behind Blue, who had reached the reservoir and was lowering his head to take a drink.

When they finally drew closer, Christina turned Star's head toward the water. But just as he reached the water's edge, he turned sharply and planted his hooves.

"Oh, here we go again," Christina groaned, opening her rein and touching her heel behind the girth in an effort to turn him back.

She was conscious of Lyssa's watchful eye as Star balked once more, flattening his ears.

"Is he afraid of water?" Lyssa asked.

Christina shook her head. "Never has been."

"Then I'm right. He's pushing you away. Don't let him do that. Ride him straight into that water, right up to his neck, and let him argue with you where neither of you can get hurt."

Christina shook her head. What was Lyssa talking about? "I'm not riding him into that freezing water."

"You've got to grab the moment. Right now, getting him to listen to you is the important thing. It's sunny. He'll dry off," Lyssa said.

Christina bit her lip and hesitated.

"Do it, right now. Don't give him any more time to cross you. This is your chance to let him battle it out and get him to realize you're on his side."

"No. I'll let him have a drink, but that's it. Who knows how deep that water is."

"I'll tell you how deep it is—not more than four feet at the center. See that measuring stick right there in the middle? Now go."

Christina took both reins in one hand and swung

her leg over Star, dropping to the ground.

"Uh, would you mind telling me what you're doing?" Lyssa asked.

Christina didn't meet her eyes as she turned and led Star back down the way they'd come. "I'm leading Star back to his stall," she said quietly.

"Hell-*o*! You're supposed to be riding that horse—into that water!"

Christina gritted her teeth. "I really appreciate what you're trying to do, Lyssa, but I can't risk getting him hurt or sick again. I didn't come all the way to Montana for that!" she blurted out. "Anyway, you're nuts if you think taking Star for a swim is going to change anything!"

8

"SO YOU THINK I'M NUTS, HUH? WELL, TELL THAT TO THE Native Americans. They've used water for training their horses for centuries!" Lyssa snapped. "If you ask me, you're the one who's nuts, coming all the way here just to turn up your nose at every suggestion!"

Christina answered with a glare.

With that, Lyssa shrugged. "Suit yourself. But if you'll excuse me, I don't have all day to hang around here watching this loser tug-of-war game you're playing. I have work to do. If you need me, I'll be around."

Christina watched Lyssa set off through the pasture, then turned back to Star, feeling hot tears well up. She was tempted to call Lyssa back, but there didn't seem to be any point. There was no way she was going to do something as dumb as ride a valuable racehorse like Star up to his neck into a reservoir!

A half hour later Christina returned to the barn with Star, exhausted from cajoling him all the way back. She clipped his lead to the eyebolt in the wall and groomed him thoroughly. Then she stood back to admire her work.

"Well, you *look* better and better every day," she said, trying to bolster her spirits.

Out of habit, she began massaging Star, starting at his poll and working down toward his withers and along his topline. While she worked, she glanced around the dim interior of the barn. The afternoon sun shone weakly through a window, and she could see the puppies nursing in the straw by the tractor wheel. B.C. was dozing in the doorway. She could hear the laughter of the guests drift in. Everyone and everything on this cozy, friendly ranch seemed to be content. Why was she so miserable?

"There now, doesn't that feel good?" she murmured, leaning close to Star as she rubbed his shoulder, taking in his special scent of horse and hay.

"Hey, I *thought* I was on a ranch, but I guess I've stepped into a day spa instead," said Ray with a creepy laugh. Christina smiled politely, wishing he would go away.

"You sure do spoil that horse," Ray added, looking Star up and down and tucking his thumbs into his belt loops.

"Maybe I do," Christina said evenly. "But he deserves to be spoiled."

Mitch came in just then. After glancing at Christina, he said to Ray, "Hey, Ray, the guys are looking for you to play horseshoes with them. Go join 'em."

Ray hesitated, but he left. Turning back to Christina, Mitch watched her massage Star for a moment.

"You know, there's an empty turnout pen right behind the barn. Why don't you grab it while you can and let your horse go drink up a little Montana sunshine? We won't be having much more of that around here for a while."

"Thanks, I think I will," said Christina gratefully.

A few minutes later she was leaning against the rails, watching Star. She wasn't expecting much. The way he was acting lately, she figured he'd probably just stand around in his disinterested way and wait to be put back in his stall. Christina was surprised when he set out at a brisk pace along the rail, with his nose to the ground, kicking up dirt. Folding his front legs, he sank to the ground, rolling from side to side in the dirt. The next minute he was up, snorting and arching his neck. Picking up an animated trot, he shot around the enclosure.

Now why couldn't you act like that when I was riding you this morning? Christina thought, shaking her head.

She didn't know how long she stood there, riveted, as Star played like a foal, staging mock battles with his forefeet one moment, then flaring his nostrils and trumpeting so loudly, Christina was sure they could hear him all the way to Billings.

As she stared, her heart swelled with pride. The old Star was still in there somewhere. But what had happened to him during his illness to change everything?

"Aha," said Mitch, suddenly appearing at her elbow. "You're like me; you study horses. I can watch my Cody for hours. There's nothing like it. You can really get to know a horse that way."

Christina continued to gaze at Star. "I've had Star since he was born. I like to watch him, but I already know him inside and out."

"Okay, then, what's he telling you?" Mitch prodded, giving her a dose of penetrating brown eyes.

"Not much," Christina admitted. "I don't seem to be able to read him lately."

"That's because you're not speaking his language."

"Now you sound like Lyssa!" Christina burst out.

The young ranch hand shoved his fists into the pockets of his jeans. "Maybe. But she knows what she's talking about."

Christina turned her head. At that moment she

really didn't want to hear any more about Lyssa or her bizarre ideas.

"Hey, Mitch. You promised you'd show us how to rope," Cameron, one of the twins, said walking up behind them.

Christina noted that a stampede string was dangling from her hat, and she smiled.

"Oh," Cameron exclaimed when she saw Star. "That horse is so pretty."

As Caitlin peered around the corner, Cameron motioned her over. "This is the kind of horse I want one day," she announced.

"Naw, Cameron," Mitch teased, winking at Christina. "If you want to learn to rope cattle, you'd better get a quarter horse. Best horses in the whole world."

Christina entered into the game. "Do you like to ride fast?" she asked Cameron.

"Yes," the girls chorused.

"That settles it, then. A Thoroughbred," Christina said, grinning at Mitch.

"So it's true, you really are a jockey?" asked Caitlin, looking more closely at her.

Christina nodded, feeling her cheeks flame. She certainly didn't feel like a jockey anymore. She could barely make her horse trot.

"I'll come watch you race one day," breathed the girl.

Christina nodded self-consciously and glanced at Mitch.

"Come on, let's go rope. The others are waiting," Mitch said. He tipped his hat to Christina and walked off with the girls.

After Christina settled Star back into his stall, she surveyed the equipment lying around. Everyone else seemed to be busy around here. She might as well pitch in and help out as well.

Setting the dusty brushes in a bucket of soapy water, Christina picked up the lead ropes that were flopped on the tractor and hung them on pegs by the medicine cabinet. Turning her attention to the piles of dirty bridles, she picked up a bar of glycerin saddle soap and sat on the tractor seat to clean the leather. After the bridles were clean, Christina hung them carefully over tuna fish cans that were nailed on the wall. Setting the wet brushes on the ledge outside the barn door to dry, she stopped to rest for a moment. In the distance she could see Mitch with the young guests, guiding their arms as they twirled long, snaking ropes. She watched for a moment as Lyssa joined them, standing behind the girls and placing her hands over their arms, guiding them in their throws. Marveling at Lyssa's patience, Christina saw that it didn't take long before the girls became more accurate. Soon several more guests joined them, and the competition heated up.

Moments later a group of guests rode into the corral, led by Cal. Christina automatically went up to grab horses and help guests dismount. Cal took off his cowboy hat and waved it at Christina.

"Just turned these tenderfoots into regular, bona fide cowboys," he crowed.

"I'm so saddle sore," said one of the college girls, who smiled gratefully as Christina took her horse. "I'm going to take the *longest* hot shower."

"I'm not riding that horse ever again," said one of the twelve-year-old boys. He slid off and glared at his mount, a dun-colored horse with a roached mane. "There wasn't anything to grab on to, and I almost fell off six times."

He started to walk off, leaving his horse with reins dangling. Lyssa came up behind him. "Not so fast, cowboy. That horse took you a long way today. Now it's your turn to be good to him. You can start by putting on this halter here, and follow Uncle Cal to the grooming area."

The boy scowled but did as he was told.

It was late afternoon when Christina returned to her bunk, dirty and tired. She plopped on her bed and reluctantly pulled out her textbooks. It had been easy to forget that there was life anywhere but on the Black

Thunder Ranch. Henry Clay High seemed very far away.

Christina was fast asleep, her head on her books, when Caitlin poked her head into her room to call her to dinner.

After dinner Christina asked Mrs. Hynde if she could use the phone. She sat on a scratchy Navajo rug in the hallway and punched in the number at White-brook. But the machine picked up, so she left a message saying that Star was fine and that everything at the ranch was fantastic. Then she dialed Parker's number.

"Hello?" Christina was relieved to hear Parker's voice. The last thing she wanted was to deal with Brad or Lavinia.

"Hey, Christina! How are things out on the range?" Parker asked.

Christina swallowed. "Just fine," she lied. "Star seems to like it here. I mean, it's only been a couple of days, but so far so good. I took him out today, and he seemed right at home."

"That's great. So he's acting better, huh? And Lyssa's helping you sort him out?"

"Yeah. Oh, Parker, you wouldn't believe how beautiful it is here. There's always so much to do," Christina said, skipping past the subject of Star's behavior. Normally she told Parker everything. But somehow, admitting that Star wasn't miraculously cured seemed overwhelming to Christina. Saying it aloud would make it all too real.

Instead, Christina launched into detailed descriptions of the horses and the guests and Lyssa and Blue. After she hung up, she was conscious that she hadn't been totally truthful. That night she lay awake for a long time, tossing and turning and trying to get comfortable in her strange bed.

"Oh, so you're hungry after all your adventures yesterday, huh?" Christina asked Star the next morning, watching him bob his head impatiently as she mixed up his feed.

Lyssa came down the barn aisle with a wheelbarrow of soiled bedding. "Morning," she said brightly. "You're up early."

"Not really," Christina said.

Christina was grateful that Lyssa didn't seem mad at her anymore. She might not want to do everything Lyssa told her to do with Star, but she didn't want them to be enemies.

"How's Star?" Lyssa asked.

Christina shrugged. "As good as can be expected."

Lyssa pushed back some hair that had escaped from her silver barrette. "Well, the Johnsons asked if a

110

few of us could come over and help them vaccinate today. They've got a backlog of work on their ranch. Mr. Johnson is the guy who taught me dressage. I owe him everything. Want to come?"

"Sure," Christina said hesitantly, glancing at Star.

"Great," said Lyssa. "We'll leave right after breakfast, and we'll be back by noon, so you'll have plenty of time for Star."

Christina smiled. "Sounds good."

An hour later she was rattling along the road toward Three Creek Ranch in the back of the pickup truck, along with Lyssa and the twins. Cal, Mitch, and Ray were up front in the cab, and Christina was glad she didn't have to sit next to Ray.

"You'll like the Johnsons," Lyssa told her. "Mr. Johnson and my dad have known each other since they were babies. And their little grandkids, Dusty and Skye, are so cute on their ponies!"

As they topped the hill, Christina could see the wooden frame of Three Creek's signpost. Christina felt a blast of cold wind hit her face, and she looked up at the gray sky.

Lyssa was gazing up, too. "We'd better step on it. Looks like rain."

"Too bad," Christina said.

But Lyssa shook her head. "Not really. We don't get much rain here. Mostly it rains on the other side of the

Rockies. So what we get we're grateful for—as long as it doesn't turn into snow."

"Thanks for helping out, Lyssa," said a thin, older man when they pulled up outside the corral. His face was dark with dirt and sunburn, his voice deep. He tipped his hat briefly to Christina and then turned back to the bucket he was filling with medication and syringes.

"That's Skip Johnson," Lyssa whispered to Christina. "I brought you a bunch of helpers," she called out to him.

"So I see," Mr. Johnson said, his lips moving while he counted. "They can help us move the cattle back into the pens after we've vaccinated them. Maybe a couple of your guests wouldn't mind helping man the barbecue pit. We'll show everyone some real Western hospitality after the work's all done."

Lyssa pointed at a grassy area next to the house where several long trestle tables had been set up. They were covered with red-and-white cloths held down by horseshoes. Christina could see a woman bustling around the fire pit, from which smoke was billowing into the air. "No one ever leaves this ranch hungry," Lyssa said. "If I know Mrs. Johnson, she's got enough food to feed half the state."

Christina smiled, but she couldn't help hoping that the barbecue wouldn't take too long. She had already made up her mind that she wanted to take Star up to Lyssa's dressage arena, away from reservoirs and bulls. Maybe if she could just work him slowly in small circles, he'd start focusing and she could get him to start paying attention to her again.

After Lyssa conferred with a couple of the hands and everyone was assigned to a task, she and Christina went back to where Mr. Johnson was marking some numbers on his clipboard.

"Let's see now. The boys have already brought the first group down," Johnson said. "We need to get them in the chute and give them each a couple of sub-Qs."

"Sub-Qs?" Christina was puzzled.

"Subcutaneous injections," Lyssa explained. "Just under the skin."

Christina absorbed this. "Don't you have vets to do it?"

Lyssa shrugged. "Nah. This is routine. We only call in the vets for the serious stuff."

Mr. Johnson glanced over to the pen, where a couple of hands were herding cattle toward a metal chute. It was clear that more help was needed, as several cattle scattered and broke away. "Why don't you two go get Minnie and Maggie, saddle them up, and help bring down the next group. I'll send some people out there to help my wranglers get this group in the chute."

"Sure thing," Lyssa said. "So how's Minnie doing with the trailering these days?"

Mr. Johnson's craggy face split into a grin. "I don't know how you did it. That old she-devil hasn't wanted to go near a trailer for years. One week with you, and now she loads like a baby."

He turned to Christina. "This girl, she's got a way with horses."

I know, I know, Christina thought. *That's what everyone tells me.*

Following Lyssa up a steep slope to Minnie and Maggie's corral, Christina helped halter the two Appaloosa mares.

Christina lifted the heavy Western saddle onto Maggie and tightened the cinch. After she swung her leg over the little mare, Christina shifted in the saddle, trying to get comfortable, and closed her hands tentatively on the rawhide hackamore Lyssa had slipped over the mare's head.

"Careful with that thing," Lyssa said, frowning at the hackamore. "It's called a bosal, and it's more severe than it looks."

Christina decided to let the reins rest on the mare's neck. She didn't want to chance hurting a horse with a piece of equipment she didn't understand.

Moments later they had made their way up a path behind the feed barn, where they joined two other hands who were rounding up a group of cattle.

One short guy who was mounted on a chalk white horse motioned them on either side of the throng of white-faced Herefords. "You two flank 'em. I'll ride point and Kelli will ride drag," he shouted as he opened the gate.

"That means Bob goes to the front, Kelli goes to the back, and we each take a side," Lyssa explained, giving a sharp "Yee-ah!" and shooting to the right.

"But wait! What do I do?" yelped Christina.

I guess I'd better figure it out in a hurry, she thought as Lyssa disappeared into a cloud of dust. The next minute Christina was nearly unseated as Maggie darted to the left, then shot forward.

That's it, Christina thought with relief. *Maggie knows what to do!*

Maggie snaked in and out of the cattle as they poured out of the corral and down the hill toward the parking area. The handy little mare shifted her weight forward and dropped her shoulders, every so often reaching out to nip a wayward steer.

Christina found she had no choice but to sit deep with her legs sticking out in front of her. *This is like riding a twister,* she decided, choking on the dust.

A few moments later Christina heard an incredibly loud clap of thunder. Seconds after that, the heavens unleashed a torrent of rain, instantly sending dirt and water down her face.

"Whoa, girl," Christina said uneasily. She didn't like being on a strange horse in this kind of weather, and the situation was growing more chaotic by the moment.

Maggie didn't seem to mind the sudden weather change. But the cattle mooed more urgently, shoving and trying to leap over each other. They began to crowd Maggie, who laid her ears flat and lowered her head.

"Hold 'em, hold 'em!" shouted Lyssa.

Just then a huge bolt of lightning lit up the sky, bathing the area in an eerie light.

"They're breaking your way," shouted Bob.

Before Christina could form the word *stampede* in her brain, she could feel the momentum shift. The cattle turned toward Lyssa, who started desperately trying to head them off. Christina could see her riding for dear life on a snaking, darting Minnie, who wheeled and spun and seemed to be everywhere at once.

Christina wanted to help, but she realized her job was to hold the left line at all costs. Her eyes never left Lyssa, and she was mesmerized by the determination in Lyssa's face as she zipped back and forth, quickly bringing the unruly cattle back under control.

It was over in only a few seconds, and when the group was herded into the holding pen, none the worse for wear, Christina let out a huge sigh. Lyssa rode over to her and tipped her rain-soaked hat.

"That was amazing," Christina exclaimed. "I've never seen anything like that!"

Lyssa grinned. "All in a day's work!"

"Well done, Lyssa," shouted Bob, dashing over to them on his soaked gelding, whose white coat was now flecked with mud. "Wonder Girl does it again!"

Two hours later Christina carried a heaping plate of food over to a table that had been hastily moved inside a low tractor shed when the rain came.

"That was fun," Christina said, sliding into her seat next to Mr. Johnson. "I loved riding in that thunderstorm."

Mr. Johnson grinned. "Well, we got the work done anyway, no thanks to the weather. I'm mighty grateful for your help," he said, biting into a rib smothered in barbecue sauce.

Christina glanced across the shed to where Mitch had set up a chair and a microphone. Soon he started strumming a guitar and playing requests, mostly country tunes that Christina recognized from listening to the radio on the way to Montana. Every so often the Johnsons' grandchildren, Dusty and Skye, would grab the mike and say silly things, but no one seemed to mind.

As Christina ate she looked around at the tables crowded with dirty, muddy people laughing, eating, and enjoying themselves. She smiled to herself as she thought of the Townsends' party she had gone to only a few days before. That elegant affair had been so different from this one, but Christina couldn't help feeling that she was enjoying this one more, apart from missing Parker. She couldn't help picturing the look of horror on Lavinia's face if her dinner guests dared wear muddy, soaked jeans and soggy cowboy boots to one of her parties.

"What are you smiling at?" asked Ray, squeezing in next to her.

Christina shook her head. "Oh, nothing," she said. Would Ray never leave her alone? Glancing up, she saw Lyssa over at the next table wiggle her eyebrows at her, and she had to look away before she burst into laughter.

"How's that horse of yours?" Ray asked. "Given up on him yet?"

Instantly Christina's mood shifted, and she felt guilty for being away for so long playing cowboy when she should have been back at the Black Thunder concentrating on Star.

"He's doing all right," she said firmly, eating a forkful of potato salad. *If only that were true,* she added to herself.

Christina ignored Ray as he began to brag about the death-defying stunts he'd pulled that day. With his voice droning on in the background, Christina considered her next move with Star. It was dawning on her that even if she did take Star up to the dressage arena, chances were he wouldn't do a thing she asked. Where would that get her?

Looking up, Christina watched Lyssa eat and laugh with the ranch hands she'd known all her life. She couldn't help thinking that even though they all knew what they were doing when it came to horses, they respected Lyssa's advice. And the paying guests were all in awe of Lyssa, treating her like some cowgirl goddess of the West. She could do no wrong.

Suddenly it was all clear. Christina was one of the city slickers, too, except she was even worse because she refused to listen to anyone or try anything new. At least that was true where Star was concerned. She was the one who had been wasting precious time, blowing off Lyssa's helpful advice. Sure, some of Lyssa's suggestions were pretty wild, but they were Star's only chance!

9

AFTER THEY RETURNED TO THE BLACK THUNDER, CHRISTINA tacked up Star while Lyssa jumped on Blue. Then the girls headed to the dressage arena, where Lyssa watched Christina walk and trot for a few moments, and then told her to dismount.

"I want to try something here," Lyssa said. "It's called fingertip yielding. It's a way of building a respect system with your horse while you're on the ground. We'll start by backing Star up. Press your palm here. This should cause Star to back."

She demonstrated, pointing to an area on the bridge of Star's nose. Christina pushed with the palm of her hand. Star stood without moving.

"Okay," said Lyssa, frowning a little. "Let's go to phase two."

Lyssa then had Christina push her thumb and middle finger alongside the bridge of the horse's nose. Star backed, but without any real energy. Lyssa showed Christina a few more fingertip yield points that she could try later on her own, then had her mount again and do a series of trot-to-canter transitions broken up by halts.

"I want Star shifting gears constantly. We're trying to unbalance him a little," Lyssa explained. "This way he'll be more likely to try to pay attention to what you want him to do rather than start zoning out the way he's been doing lately."

Christina bit her lip. She tried applying her aids precisely, but it really wasn't working. Star would either run into the canter, pulling on her hands, or refuse to stop once he got started.

"Remember, it's all about baby steps," Lyssa said when they finished. "You don't want to rush or push Star. It'll just make him resist you more."

Resist me more? Christina thought, discouraged. *How is that possible?*

On Monday morning Christina had just started toward the barn when the soft strains of Mozart reached her ears.

"Classical music?" she exclaimed, trying to figure out where it was coming from.

It was still dark, and from across the road she could see Lyssa trotting Blue in circles in the dressage arena. Several lights tied to wooden posts were doing a barely adequate job of lighting up the area. And sitting on top of a pile of straw bales was a large boom box that was the source of the sound.

Lyssa's doing a musical freestyle! Christina realized. Freestyle, Christina knew, was an elegant form of dressage in which horse and rider teams did a series of dressage movements in time to music. Up to now, dressage riders had performed freestyle routines in exhibitions and at some dressage shows, but recently freestyle had been approved as an Olympic event. Since such routines weren't part of a three-day event, Christina had had no idea that Lyssa knew much about them.

Huh, she thought. *Lyssa is definitely full of surprises.*

Drawing closer, Christina was surprised to see that Lyssa was riding in a deep dressage saddle and full bridle. What's more, she was dressed in beige breeches, perfectly polished dressage boots, and a crisp white shirt. And in contrast to the reddish dirt and hilly terrain found everywhere else, the arena was perfectly flat, with rich, dark footing. The horse-and-rider team looked startlingly formal against the backdrop of the ranch.

Christina felt herself drawn in as she watched

Lyssa take Blue through a series of circles and serpentines at a sitting trot that was perfectly timed to the music. Lyssa sat effortlessly in the saddle, her cues invisible. Soon the tempo of the music changed, and Blue picked up a collected canter and executed a series of lead changes in perfect time. Christina's throat tightened as she saw how effortlessly horse and rider were communicating.

After she finished, Lyssa let out her reins to reward him, and Blue dropped his head. They made their way over to where Christina was standing.

"Wow," Christina said, reaching up to pat the flea-bitten gray's neck. "He definitely looks like Olympic material."

Lyssa grinned, taking off her black gloves and stuffing them in the back pocket of her breeches. "Thanks. I hope so. It was a good work." Sliding off her horse, she leaned over to shut off the boom box.

"But why were you tacked up? Don't you usually school without it?" Christina was perplexed.

"Normally I do. But today I decided Blue needed me to shake things up a bit. Lately I've fallen back into the habit of schooling in chaps and riding him on the wire. It's easy for him to become complacent and anticipate everything." She pulled at Blue's enormous ears affectionately. "Then he starts tuning me out."

Christina had the uncomfortable feeling that Lyssa was actually dropping a huge hint in her direction.

Lyssa paused before she said nonchalantly, "I've got some time after breakfast. What do you say you get on Star and go for a stroll? Dad wants me to check some fences up by the north pasture. The ground is pretty good over there, so it won't put any strain on Star's legs."

"No reservoirs?" Christina said with extra emphasis.

"No reservoirs, although I still think it wouldn't have hurt Star to thrash out whatever's bothering him. Water's a pretty nice cushion."

"Thanks, but no thanks."

It was one thing to decide to be more open to Lyssa's suggestions. But when it came to her water trick, that was where Christina drew the line!

After breakfast Christina met Lyssa at the corral. She was riding a pretty palomino that nickered like crazy at the other horses in the corral.

"Lady's getting pretty barn sour," Lyssa explained, adjusting the wire around the mare's neck as Christina rode up to her on Star. "She's like a lot of the horses around here. Every so often I have to remind her she can't take advantage of our guests."

As they cut across the dirt road that led past the

buggy shed, Christina sucked in the clean coolness of the air and tried to lose herself in the simple pleasure of being on horseback. Maybe if she just relaxed in the saddle and didn't get all tense, Star would forget about acting up and get back to business.

Looking around, Christina caught sight of a smooth, flat stretch she hadn't seen before. There were a number of broken-down brush jumps laid out at intervals. "What's that?" she asked, pointing.

"That's where I used to practice steeplechase," Lyssa said. "That was before Cal made a deal with a small racetrack nearby. He said I'd break my fool neck out here with all the rabbit holes."

Well, it's a good thing Star is going slowly, then, Christina thought, looking down every so often at the ground. It didn't make sense to ignore the footing and risk injuring him, she told herself.

As they rode along, Christina sensed a gradual shift in Star's attitude. Though still sulky, he was now becoming increasingly resistant. First he lashed out with his hind leg when she touched his side with her heel. Then he raised his head to evade the bit when she tried to slow him just before a steep dip in the trail they were following.

"I think he's still a little edgy out here in the open," she said as he threw in a little buck when they went past a water trough.

Lyssa stopped and shielded her eyes against the sun. "I hate to disagree, but I think he's had enough excuses. Anytime you try to communicate with him, he blocks it out, plain and simple. No getting around it—he needs to join up with you again."

Christina furrowed her brow. "Join up?"

"It's a term some horse trainers use. It means the horse voluntarily decides to team up with a human."

"I have news for you. Star and I are already a team!"

"*Were* a team," Lyssa said softly. "Now, don't get mad at me."

Christina looked down at the ground. "Fine. So what do I do now?" she asked. "Besides plunging into a reservoir. You can forget that."

"Well, I have another idea," Lyssa said. "I have to head off tomorrow to round up a couple of geldings left up at the summer pasture. It's a few miles from here, near the base of the Beartooth Mountains. We'd have to be gone overnight. I was going to go up with Aunt Gwen, but why don't you and Star come along instead? We could pack our supper and cook it over a campfire. We'll sleep out at the station up there. It'll do Star some good to sleep out on the open range, under the stars."

"I don't see how going camping will accomplish anything."

Lyssa's sky blue eyes scanned the seemingly endless horizon, sweeping back and forth in that way Christina knew so well now. Her voice seemed to come from far away as she said, "It's about making him want to come back to you. Take away his normal environment, his friends, his habits, and he'll turn to the one thing that's still left to him: That's you. Don't you see?"

Lyssa evidently thought it was reasonable, but Christina wasn't buying it. It sounded more like a fairy tale than real life. And anyway, it seemed a little more rugged than she was ready for.

"Uh-uh. Star's not a range horse. He's used to being pampered. We're talking snug barns at night and civilization. Coming here was strange enough for him."

Lyssa toyed with the wire loop around Lady's neck. "There you go again!" she said, shaking her head.

"There I go again what?"

"Shaking off everything I say. You've got to trust me, Christina, or your whole trip out here is just a huge waste. You might as well go back to Kentucky if you're not going to give me a chance."

Christina was getting annoyed. Lyssa could be so obstinate sometimes, and she was tired of it. "There could be bears or snakes or mountain lions," she insisted. But the minute she said it, she wished she hadn't.

"Not to mention rabid, horse-eating elks," Lyssa added mischievously. "Carnivorous mutant kangaroos just waiting to feast on unsuspecting racehorses."

"Will you stop it with the dumb jokes? This whole thing could ruin Star forever!"

"*Or* it could be just the thing he needs," Lyssa said, getting serious again. "Either way, you're gambling on his future. Do you want to go back to Whitebrook and tell everyone you were too wimpy to try to help Star?"

"That's not fair!" Christina flashed.

But Lyssa wasn't listening. She had ridden up to the break in the fence and was leaning over with her wire cutters, concentrating on repairing the broken wire.

Christina was just about to ask if she needed any help when Star whirled around, facing the way they had come.

"Oh, no you don't," Christina said, setting her jaw.

She succeeded in turning Star back in the right direction, but the effort caused her to break out in a sweat, even though the air was still and cold.

She stood silently while Lyssa finished twisting wires, and on the way back neither of them brought up the subject of the overnight. But when Star balked at the small creek they'd crossed on their way up, Christina felt herself caving.

128

"If we *did* go, let's just say, would you take Blue?"

"Probably not," she said. "I can't afford to mess up his schedule just now. He needs his fitness gallops, and the trail to the station doesn't fit that bill. I'll probably take this girl. She's a packer and a half."

"Who rides Blue when you can't?"

"Uncle Cal. Or sometimes I let Mitch ride him."

Christina pursed her lips and finally gave in. "Fine. I'll go," she said.

"Good," said Lyssa. Then she started humming again in a self-satisfied way that made Christina want to scream.

Oh, Star, I hope we're doing the right thing, she muttered to herself later as she untacked him and started rubbing him down.

"Got a duster?" said Lyssa, scanning the sky on Tuesday afternoon as they made last-minute preparations for their trip.

Christina looked up from the thin roll of bedding stuffed with a change of clothes she was tying onto the back of a saddle Lyssa had lent her. She eyed the other girl blankly. "A duster?"

"It's like a canvas jacket. It goes all the way down your legs to protect you from the wind and weather while you ride. Everyone around here uses them when we go for any distance. You never know what you'll run into as you get closer to the mountains."

"I don't need any more clothes, that's for sure. I've got so many layers as it is, I feel like a blimp," Christina joked. "Anyway, I'm trying to keep things as light as I can. Star's getting stronger and stronger every day, but he's definitely not a packhorse."

"Well, he'd certainly be the most gorgeous packhorse anyone's seen around here in a while," said Lyssa.

She's just trying to butter me up because she knows I don't want to go, Christina thought sourly.

"Hey, Mitch," Lyssa said as he opened the gate behind them. "Lend Christina here your duster, okay? I think we might head into some weather."

"Sure thing." Mitch nodded. He motioned to the saddlebag he'd brought with him from the house. "Your mom says you'd better not leave without something to eat. I checked it out on the way down, and I'm jealous. Rocks and some leftover train wreck. You're good to go."

Christina glanced at the saddlebag with alarm. "Don't look so worried," Lyssa said, laughing. "Rocks are beef cubes wrapped in dough with onions and potatoes. They'll taste great cooked over a campfire for breakfast tomorrow."

"And train wreck?" said Christina, not quite convinced.

"Dinner. It's Mrs. Hynde's special chili-and-tortilla-chip concoction. The best," Mitch assured her. He ducked into the barn and emerged with a folded duster, which he flipped to Christina. She took it reluctantly and draped it in front of her saddle.

"Lady's pretty loaded up here. Mind if we hitch the food onto Star's saddle?" Lyssa asked Christina.

Christina wasn't happy about adding any more weight to Star, but she decided she was going a little overboard. The food didn't weigh that much. Leaning over, she started fastening on Star's bell boots and cannon boots.

While Mitch tied on the small bag, he glanced down. "What's with all the fancy footgear?"

Christina shrugged. "I don't want Star to get cut up by sagebrush or barbed wire."

Mitch snorted. "You easterners worry too much."

Lyssa glanced at Christina and then said, "Uh, Mitch, would you mind going back up to the house and asking my mom to remember to feed the puppies for me?"

Mitch knew he was being dismissed. He tipped his hat playfully at both of them and turned on his heel. "Watch out for grizzlies," he called.

Grizzlies? Christina wondered fearfully. Then she scolded herself. *Get a grip. Lyssa knows what she's doing.*

"Sounds like an adventure," Ashleigh had said when Christina telephoned after dinner the night before to tell her about her plans. Christina had made light of it, all the while hoping it actually wouldn't turn out to be too much of an adventure.

Finally Christina was ready, and she mounted up.

Star snorted and tossed his head. *At least he's in high spirits,* Christina thought, feeling slightly encouraged.

Lyssa mounted Lady and neck-reined her in front of Star.

"We're off," she cried, her saddle creaking.

Christina wished she could share Lyssa's enthusiasm. *Oh, I'd give anything to be home safe and sound,* she thought as she fell in behind Lady. Things would be quiet at Whitebrook about now. The barn chores would be done until feeding time. She and Melanie would be hanging out together, maybe catching up on some homework or thumbing through old *Bloodhorse* magazines. Or maybe she'd hack over to Whisperwood and help Parker give lessons.

Stop it, Christina commanded herself.

As they rode up onto the dirt road in front of the main house, Christina saw Gwen and Cal draw up by the bunkhouse in a wooden hay wagon pulled by two sturdy-looking bay draft horses with feathered fetlocks and feet that seemed twice as big as Blue's.

"I almost forgot. It's hayride day," Lyssa said, her eyes resting affectionately on the big horses. "That's Doc and Sleepy."

Cal jumped off and started loading people into the wagon. As everyone settled in they turned to wave to Lyssa and Christina.

"Hope you'll all think of us while we're out on the trail eating rocks," Lyssa said, wiggling her eyebrows at the children who were perched high on the hay bales.

"Rocks?" asked Caitlin. "Yuck!"

"Take good care of Blue while we're gone," Lyssa called to her uncle.

Uncle Cal gave her a thumbs-up sign.

Lyssa squeezed her heels into Lady, and they set off. As Christina waved goodbye to everybody, she was surprised to feel a pang at leaving the ranch. Up to now, the Black Thunder had seemed so different and strange, but now that she was heading off into the wild, it felt safe and familiar.

"We have to go along the main road to get to the trail, but it's a short way, and the truckers are pretty respectful of riders," Lyssa called over her shoulder.

Trucks? Oh, great, Christina groaned silently. *If my parents or Ian saw me riding Star next to a highway, they'd kill me!*

Christina followed Lyssa and turned Star onto the shoulder of the road leading to the main road. The sun was high overhead, but it wasn't giving off much warmth. Christina was thankful for the thick down

133

jacket she'd borrowed from Gwen for the trip. Several semis rolled past on the highway, but apart from flicking his ears, Star gave no sign that he was concerned. Christina patted his shoulder reassuringly, and shortly they turned off the highway, making their way up a steep little path that wound its way along the creek bed.

"Around this little rise is an abandoned schoolhouse my grandfather went to when he was a boy," Lyssa said.

Through a stand of stunted trees planted as a windbreak, Christina caught a glimpse of a graying wooden building that leaned precariously. She wished she had thought to bring a camera. It would have been fun to have a picture to show her friends.

As they rode on, Christina started to relax. The terrain wasn't too bad, and Star seemed to be keeping up with Lady's short, even strides. Every so often he'd catch a scent and flare his nostrils, and though he was still lackluster, he wasn't being disobedient.

"So tell me, how come you trust a cowboy like Mitch to ride Blue for you?" Christina asked conversationally. She'd been surprised to hear Lyssa would let someone like him get on her highly trained Olympic horse.

Lyssa's eyes danced. "Don't let appearances deceive you. He might look like your typical rough-ridin' cowboy, but he's one of the truest natural horsemen I know."

Then she looked at Christina in a way that confirmed what Christina already knew. Christina couldn't help asking, "You're crazy for him, aren't you?"

"I'll never tell," Lyssa said, her cheeks turning bright red. Quickly she turned the question. "And what's with you and Ray? I see him checking you out."

Christina snorted so loudly, Lady threw up her head and rolled her eyes suspiciously. "Don't make me gag!" she said.

Lyssa laughed. "Well, don't worry. He's heading back home tomorrow, and he'll be gone by the time we come back. Oh, my achy breaky heart," she twanged in her best country-western warble.

"Thank goodness," Christina said, giggling. "Eee-yew!"

After a while conversation ceased between them when the trails became narrower and they had to ride single file toward the low hills in front of them.

They had been riding for a couple of hours when Christina became aware that the sky was darkening. A slight wind picked up, propelling a few tumbleweeds past them.

"Well, well. More rain," Lyssa said as a few sprinkles landed on them.

"You said it didn't rain much around here. You don't think it'll get much worse, do you?" Christina asked. "Star isn't used to being out in storms."

135

Lyssa brushed the raindrops off her face and shook her head. "Naw. It's nothing. But it's time to break out the dusters if you don't want to get soaked," she said matter-of-factly just as the drops began splattering them.

The rain became steady, and the girls dismounted long enough to unpack rainproof dusters that they put on over their clothes.

Lyssa motioned to a craggy canyon to their left. "It's not that much farther. We'll go up to the rise, then take the fork and we're there."

Christina nodded miserably, thankful that at least the temperature hadn't dropped much. She didn't want Star catching a cold.

The next minute she heard a clap of thunder. Star shied so violently, Christina was thrown up on his shoulder.

"Easy there, big guy," she said soothingly.

She glanced at Lady, who didn't seem to notice the thunder. She and Lyssa continued up the winding path as if nothing happened.

"See, Star? Nothing to worry about," Christina crooned, patting his damp coat.

"I don't know about you, but I'm getting a little tired of this. Let's make some tracks," Lyssa said suddenly, clucking loudly to Lady. The palomino broke into a trot and disappeared around a huge boulder.

Just then Star slammed on his brakes and refused to budge. "Oh, Star, not now, please. Wait, Lyssa, slow down," Christina called. She was about to dig her heels into Star's sides when a bolt of lightning split the sky.

Star seemed to jump straight up in the air, throwing Christina sideways in her saddle. Then another flash of lightning lit up the sky, illuminating the great boulder in front of her.

Christina tightened her hold on the reins and tried to right herself. The next instant, as Star took a step, his feet went out from under him in the slick mud and he fell on his side.

She braced herself for the pain as eleven hundred pounds of Star came crashing down upon her.

10

"CHRISTINA, ARE YOU ALL RIGHT?" SHOUTED LYSSA AS SHE dashed from behind the boulder.

Christina lay stunned for a few seconds as she became aware that, contrary to what she'd expected, she wasn't hurt. Amazingly, the big colt had fallen so that her leg was pinned right under the indentation behind his shoulder, just before the place where his ribs swelled. He scrambled up without stepping on her, and she rolled away, gasping for breath, as Star stood up and shook himself off.

Christina got up shakily, wiping the mud from her cheek, then rushed over to check Star's legs. She couldn't see any cuts or scrapes, and as far as she could tell, he wasn't hurt. Leading Star in a small circle, she turned to watch his steps. He seemed fine.

"Talk about lucky," she said, her heart still pounding from her near miss.

Lyssa hurried over and stood next to her anxiously. Her face was white. Neither of them said anything for a moment while Christina rubbed her hands over Star one more time, checking again for any signs of injury.

"He's okay," she said finally. "I can't believe it, considering the way he fell."

"You want to go on or turn back?" Lyssa's voice, though soft, was a challenge.

Christina looked down at her muddy clothes, then at Star. "I can't believe I'm saying this," she finally muttered. "Let's go on."

Adjusting her bedroll and the food bag, Christina climbed back on the muddy saddle. "Well, I guess now it's mud with rocks for breakfast tomorrow. Yum, yum," she joked weakly.

Lyssa had her face tilted toward the sky, the water pouring off her hat and down her back. "All right," she said slowly. "Plan B. There's an overhang just behind these rocks. Let's get out of this wet. We'll head off again when it lets up."

Christina nodded and followed Lyssa to the rocky overhang, where they dismounted, leading the horses under it.

Christina glanced around her in the gloomy area where they were standing. Suddenly she had a disconcerting thought. "This wouldn't by any chance be a bear cave or anything, would it?" she asked in a whisper.

"No, and there aren't any carnivorous walruses here, either," Lyssa teased. She took off her hat and brushed it off.

Scowling, Christina turned to watch the water run off the ledge overhead. "Why do you joke around so much?" she complained. "I know I'm not used to things out here, but I *am* trying, and it sure doesn't help when you kid around all the time."

Lyssa hung her head a little. "I'm sorry. I didn't know it bothered you that much. It's just a habit, I guess. We all do it to each other around the ranch, and no one takes it seriously. It's our way of trying to lighten things up when the going gets tense."

Christina absorbed this. "Yeah, well, I guess I joke around myself sometimes."

"But at least you know when to quit. I've had people tell me I get a little carried away," Lyssa replied. "I know I come on a little strong sometimes. But I sure don't mean to hurt anyone's feelings."

Neither girl said anything for a while as they listened to the rain drumming steadily, broken every so often by a rumble of thunder. The two horses stood patiently, their heads low.

"This is just like home," Lyssa said. "Sometimes we

go sit on the back porch and watch the rain. You can see the whole valley from our porch."

"Well, the view here is pretty cool, too," Christina exclaimed. "Look at the mountains. The clouds are sitting right on top of them."

"The station is just up there. We already brought down the horses we let the guests use. There are only a couple of retired geldings left. They'll be glad to come on back down the mountain. They've been up there since the beginning of summer."

Finally the rain let up, and Christina and Lyssa continued on their way. As they drew closer to the mountains, Christina was aware that the terrain was different. Where it had been vast and sparse, now it began to rise sharply, with thick pines clustered together.

Just as they reached another rise, Star pricked his ears and flared his nostrils.

"He smells the horses," Lyssa explained. "They're right over here."

A rail fence came into view as Lyssa clucked and Lady surged forward. She swung her hindquarters next to the gate while Lyssa lifted a loop of wire. Suddenly Christina felt Star's body tremble as the ground seemed to shake. Two muddy horses were hurtling toward them. They kicked up big chunks of earth, and within seconds they were at the gate, snuffling Lyssa in that jealous way Christina had seen with the ranch horses.

"Hey, guys, you're both here. Didja miss me?" Lyssa asked, leaning over and rubbing their ears. "We got lucky. This pasture is so huge, sometimes it takes a long time to locate the horses we keep here," she said to Christina. "But I guess these guys were ready to go home. We'll take them to the station and pen them for the night, and set off as soon as we break camp in the morning."

Emitting a series of low whistles, Lyssa brought her left leg well behind the cinch. Lady spun and, snaking her head low, she wheeled and darted, gathering the geldings and encouraging them toward the open gate.

"Why don't we just lead them over to the station?" Christina was mystified. "Won't they break away?"

Lyssa laughed. "Oh, believe me, they'll follow us. They know there's fresh chow waiting. Come on. I'll ride point, and you ride drag."

"Fine," said Christina, shaking her head. *They sure do things differently out here*, she thought.

She turned Star to fall in behind Lady and the geldings. But this time, for some reason, Star's racehorse instincts kicked in. No way did he want to be behind the other horses. Christina was glad to see that he hadn't lost his desire to be in front, but she couldn't help wishing he'd picked a better time to remember that he liked being the first horse to get there.

He fought her tugs on the reins, scooting up dangerously close to one dark bay.

"Not now, big guy," said Christina, closing her hand on the rein. She turned him to the right and he shot forward. As he reached the side of the trail, he turned and burst forth in the other direction, all the while keeping the geldings in front of him.

He's acting like a cutting horse! Christina realized.

Adrenaline pumping, Christina continued sweeping Star from side to side as they made their way up the trail. As she rode she felt a surge of happiness. Though they were doing something entirely new, she felt Star's old responsiveness coming through.

"We're here!" Lyssa called from the top, taking off her hat and waving it. Christina felt a stab of disappointment. It had lasted only a few moments, but she'd definitely felt it, the partnership with Star that she'd been sure she'd never feel again.

"That was unbelievable," she gasped as Lyssa slid off and opened the gate to the split-rail pen at the station. "Star thought he was a cutting horse!"

"I wish Mitch could have seen it. It might shut his mouth for a moment about quarter horse superiority," Lyssa called. "Still, I think Star would rather race."

Twisting in her saddle, she whistled sharply. Lady flattened herself against the fence as the horses rushed past. Lyssa shut the gate behind them, then turned to Christina, who had just pulled up in front of her.

"Well, this is it," she said.

There was a small shed flanked by two blackened trees and a smaller pen next to the one they'd just put the geldings in. The pens looked sturdy, and the shed appeared to have been recently built.

"We'll put Star in that pen. I'll put the food in the shed, where the bears can't get to it. And the Hotel del Campfire is just over there," Lyssa said pointing to a large fire ring made of rocks. "What do you think? Pretty luxurious, huh?"

Christina grinned. "Not bad," she said. After her thrilling ride, she was feeling pretty good. And now that they had arrived safely, she decided she could definitely be a good sport about everything—even the mention of bears. "Though what happened to those poor trees by the shed? A wildfire?"

"No," Lyssa said. "They got hit by lightning a while back."

Christina shivered. Was this the place where Blue had been struck by lightning? She decided not to ask. She couldn't imagine how horrible that must have been.

By now it was getting dark, and the sky was the color of eggplant. Watching the horses head toward the empty mangers, Christina dismounted and rubbed Star's mane.

"You were a good boy," she praised him.

"We've got just enough time to feed these guys before it's pitch black," said Lyssa, hurriedly dismounting and unsaddling Lady. She left her standing at the gate.

"Put Star in that pen, Chris. I'll feed Lady right here."

"But where will you put Lady tonight?" Christina asked.

"Oh," answered Lyssa airily, "she doesn't need a pen." Seeing Christina's look, she added, "Don't worry. You think she'd want to leave her friends and take her chances out there on the mountain by herself? Not a chance."

Shaking her head in amazement, Christina unsaddled Star and checked him one last time before putting him in the pen. Rummaging around in her pack, she found the small body brush she'd packed, along with her folding hoof pick. She cleaned out Star's hooves, removing a couple of stones that were lodged ner his frog.

"Give me a hand, will ya?" Lyssa asked, emerging from the station shed under a huge pile of hay. Christina ducked under the rail, running over and catching the pile just as it tipped. Together, the girls tossed it into the pen, where the geldings were whinnying and pawing the ground for food. Immediately the old horses fought for position, pinning their ears and giving each other nasty nips on the rump.

"Reminds me of the school cafeteria on the days they serve something good," Christina said.

145

Lyssa waved her arms. "Have some manners, boys. That's it! We're sending you down to the ranch for finishing school."

They watched the horses eat for a moment before Lyssa turned to gather some kindling for the campfire. Christina cleared the old ashes from the fire ring and piled the kindling high.

"Here are the matches," Lyssa said, tossing them to Christina. "Get that kindling going while I find a few more pieces of wood."

Before long they were sitting in front of a roaring fire, with the train wreck simmering in a foil pan over the flame.

As Christina watched the flames dance, she felt some of her earlier exhilaration seep away. It was all very nice that Star got charged up herding semiwild horses, but it was a far cry from doing what he was bred to do, racing.

"Something wrong?" asked Lyssa while she poked the fire with a long stick.

Christina shivered and moved closer to the fire. "No," she said.

They were just about to eat when Christina felt a few raindrops on her shoulders.

"Oh, no," she said. "The horses."

"Relax, it's just a light sprinkle. See? The fire's hardly going down. The horses will be fine out there," Lyssa said, removing the foil-wrapped food from the fire.

Christina looked out at the exposed pens. "But what if it rains all night?"

Lyssa shrugged, then set the food on a rock and jumped up. A few minutes later she emerged from the shed carrying a blanket for Star. "Horses have spent thousands of years sleeping in the open in far worse weather than this."

"Not Star's ancestors—well, not for a few hundred years, anyway," Christina protested, taking the water-proof blanket and walking over to put it on Star. "It's kinda small, but at least it covers him."

Lyssa's light laugh cut through the rain. "Oh, Christina, don't get all Kentucky weenie on me. Star will be fine."

"Lyssa, I'm not like you," Christina said quietly. "Our lives are different. Our horses are different. I just don't want anything to happen to Star."

"I know how much you love him, Christina," Lyssa said, her face glowing orange in the firelight. "I'd never do anything to hurt him. You've got to believe me."

Christina stared moodily into the sputtering fire as she took a few bites of the train wreck. Mitch had been right. It was pretty good, hot and just spicy enough. Too bad she didn't feel like eating.

The sprinkles let up after a while, but Christina's

mood remained depressingly low. She wandered over to Star, who was dozing contentedly in his pen, his weight on one hip.

Lyssa had just checked on the geldings when she said abruptly, "Well, I'm turning in. Tomorrow will come quickly."

"Sounds good," Christina said, all at once feeling exhausted.

She stood up and flopped her bedroll on the ground a few feet from where Lyssa had spread hers out and was changing into her nightclothes. Taking off Mitch's duster, Christina laid it over a boulder. Then, sliding under the covers, she slithered out of her riding clothes and slipped into some sweats. She layered on an extra shirt and two pairs of thick wool socks for warmth, then bunched up her heavy flannel shirt to serve as a pillow. Shivering as a coyote howled, she closed her eyes, hoping she'd fall asleep quickly.

The next morning, the sun was a pink glow over the hills as Christina opened her eyes. Stretching her stiff muscles, she stood up and glanced over at Star's pen. The gate was open, and Star wasn't there. Christina blinked. She was awake and she wasn't dreaming—Star was gone.

"Lyssa, Lyssa, get up, get up! Star's gone!" Christina's voice bubbled out of her throat as she shook Lyssa by the shoulder.

Darting over to the empty pen, she stood gaping, feeling numb all over. Her eyes locked onto the gate dangling open on a rusty hinge. *Who could have opened the gate?* she wondered wildly.

Lady, who had moved during the night to a patch of brown grass, looked around balefully. Christina's eyes were now riveted to the ground as she looked for Star's hoofprints. Unfortunately, there were a zillion hoofprints all over the place. Still wearing only her socks, she ran over to the trail, where she could see a few yards down the hillside. Star was nowhere in sight.

"Take it easy. We'll find him," Lyssa promised, coming up behind her. "He can't have gone far. And anyway, Lady's a good tracking horse."

"That's easy for you to say," Christina burst out furiously. "That's not your horse out there running around."

"Christina—" Lyssa's mouth snapped shut, and she whistled instead for Lady, who ambled over obediently, long grassy bits dangling from her mouth. "Come on, I'll saddle up and take the upper trail. You head down this way, and if we don't find Star right away, I'll meet up with you over there by those rocks."

11

"STAR, WHERE ARE YOU?" CALLED CHRISTINA, CUPPING HER hands around her mouth.

Her eyes swept over the hillside, but all she saw was scrub brush and a few rocks.

Without thinking, Christina charged down the trail in her thick socks, slipping and sliding and sending rubble tumbling down the hillside. *Where can he be?* she wondered frantically. *If anything had happened to him, she'd never forgive herself.*

I shouldn't have come out here, she told herself furiously. *I should have just stayed home. It was my fault. It was stupid, stupid, stupid!*

She whirled around as a branch snapped behind her.

"Chris, wait up."

Christina scowled as Lyssa headed toward her on Lady.

"We have to think about this," Lyssa said. "We can't just go galloping off blindly. There's an awful lot of ground to cover." She lifted her head and motioned to the vast landscape spread out below.

"All right," Christina sighed, looking down at her socks. "Where do we begin?"

"For starters, we have to go back to the station and get your shoes." Lyssa climbed off Lady and sniffed the air in a way that mystified Christina. "We also need to get you a horse, and we'll look for branches that have been broken, that sort of thing. You know, signs that anyone's been by here recently."

"But even if we find broken branches, that doesn't mean anything. They could have been broken by a bear or something. It wouldn't necessarily be Star, right?"

Lyssa nodded while climbing back on Lady. "Hey, it's a start," she said simply.

"I just don't understand how Star could get out of that pen," Christina muttered as she followed Lady up the hill and stepped on a sharp rock. "I latched it myself."

Lyssa turned around and shot Christina a guilty look. "I think it was Lady. She's the official ranch escape artist," she admitted.

"You mean she opened the gate?" Christina asked.

Lyssa nodded. "I wouldn't be surprised. I mean, there isn't anyone else around here for miles. Anyway, she's been known to do things like that before."

"Well, maybe now you'll put your horses away like most normal people do," Christina said irritably. "I think it's the dumbest thing ever to let horses run around loose like they were puppies or something."

But Lyssa wasn't paying attention. She pointed at a small path that led off from the main trail. "Look there," she said excitedly.

Christina's eyes swiveled to where she was pointing. Fresh hoofprints!

"Let's go!" she said, starting down the narrow path.

Lyssa and Lady drew up behind her as Christina followed the hoofprints for a few yards until they disappeared.

"Now what?" Christina blew out her breath, sending a wisp of her hair fluttering.

"Let's go back to the station and saddle up one of the geldings," Lyssa said. "It'll be easier to track Star on horseback than on foot."

Christina nodded, though she wasn't sure she liked the idea. After all, hadn't Lyssa told her earlier that the geldings hadn't been ridden in months? They were the nearest thing to wild horses. Under other circumstances it might be fun, but right now she didn't want to take the chance. She could just see it—she'd get bucked off a wild horse in the middle of Nowhere, Montana, while searching for her lost horse. It couldn't get any worse than that.

But what else can I do? Christina thought. It wasn't as though there were any other horses around.

"So how long has it been, exactly, since someone has ridden those horses?" she heard herself asking.

"And those gnarly claimers you ride at the tracks aren't half wild?" Lyssa fired back.

"Uh, well . . ."

Lyssa smiled. "Okay, then enough about wild horses. You can handle any of these pussycats."

Moments later Lyssa had slipped Star's bridle on the scarred, dun-colored horse and adjusted the straps to fit the horse's shorter, less refined head. "Hmmm, there's no way Star's saddle will fit old Frankystein here. He's totally mutton-withered," she said with a frown. "I'm afraid that you'll have to ride bareback." When she saw Christina's look, she added, "It's not much different from those next-to-nothing saddles you ride when you're racing."

"It's not exactly the same," Christina grumbled, eyeing the gelding's broad back. She groaned as she mounted using the bottom rail of the fence as a mounting block. Frankystein danced as she settled on his back, and she had to wrap her legs tightly around his wide barrel to keep from sliding off. "Does he rein normally or neck-rein?" Christina asked, clenching her teeth.

"Neck-rein," said Lyssa. "Don't force anything. Just talk to him. He's not a prom king or anything, but he's a really nice guy. You'll like him."

Christina wasn't so sure, but she clucked and Franky went forward obediently.

"Attaboy," Christina said, patting the horse's scarred neck. She couldn't help feeling sorry for him. "How did he get all these scars?"

Lyssa looked grim. "A pretty ugly story, actually. He'd been kept in a barbed wire pen, and his owner abused him. One day he tried to escape and got tangled in the wire. Mr. Johnson found him and bought him on the spot for twenty dollars. He brought him to me."

"Oh," said Christina, digesting this. "You poor guy."

A few minutes later Christina felt as if she'd been riding the old gelding forever. His action was much different from Star's, but he was eager to please. By the time they started down the switchback where they had seen Star's hoofprints earlier, Christina found she was completely focused.

"Okay, here we are. More fresh prints," Lyssa said suddenly.

Christina sighed with relief as she looked at the rounded imprints in the mud.

The rode on in silence until finally Lyssa spoke.

"See? I told you Franky was okay," she commented, keeping her eyes pinned to the ground. "He has a lot of cow sense—he's been on a zillion cattle drives over the years."

"Well, I hope he has some Star sense and can help us find him before he gets hurt," Christina grumbled.

"He won't have gone far," Lyssa said quietly.

Christina clung desperately to those words as they continued making their way down the mountain. The sun rose higher and higher in the sky as they rode along, stopping to examine branches and tracks. Every so often Christina would notice Lyssa sniffing the air.

What does she think she is? A bloodhound? Christina thought in disbelief. She decided not to say anything. She didn't want to hear Lyssa claiming that she could pick up Star's scent.

"I'm pretty sure we're on the right track," Lyssa said after a while. "Good thing it rained a little last night, so it's easier to tell which hoofprints are fresh."

Christina was silent, wondering just whom people called out here when horses turned up missing. The sheriffs? A posse? She was tired, sore, and worried sick. They had ridden down through a clump of trees that blocked the sun, and now, she realized, she was cold as well.

Lyssa pointed to another broken branch. "We're on his trail. We'll find him. . . . Uh-oh."

"What do you mean, uh-oh?" asked Christina, trying not to be alarmed. She didn't think she could take any more bad news.

"Fork in the trail," Lyssa exclaimed, stopping so abruptly that Lady's hindquarters tucked in underneath her. "I can't tell which way to go. Check out these pine needles; they're totally covering any prints."

"Fine," Christina snapped impatiently, slowing Franky. "You go left and I'll go right. We'll meet back here in an hour, okay?"

"That's probably not a good idea," Lyssa began, but Christina didn't stop to listen. She shot off down the right fork.

Christina kept her eyes trained to the ground, the way she'd seen Lyssa do. If only she knew more about following tracks! But it was too late to worry about that. She'd have to do the best she could.

As she rode along, she kept pushing back horrifying visions of Star injured and bleeding. She pictured him falling off a cliff, sliding down the trail and breaking a leg, or being attacked by mountain lions or bears. If only he were home at Whitebrook, safe and sound, and this was just a nightmare.

But it was no dream. It was incredibly real. The point was driven home when Christina spotted a clump of bloody copper-colored hair on a thorny bush that was growing out of the hillside just above the trail. After examining the hair and trying to ignore the blood, Christina rode on, tears threatening to blind her.

Well, at least I know Star's been this way, she thought, trying to fight down her panic. *If I find you uninjured, I'll just load you up and take you home. I don't even care anymore if you don't want to join up with me, or whatever. It'll be enough to just have you back in one piece.*

Her hopes soared as she found another clump of hair sticking to a broken branch, this time with no blood. *Star must be around here somewhere.* Suddenly she was reminded that it had been almost an hour since she'd split off from Lyssa. She'd better turn back and find her.

No way, Christina decided in the next instant. The trail was too good now. If she turned back, she'd lose more time and be that much further behind in finding Star.

Lyssa will manage, she thought, and continued on grimly, stopping only to drink from a clear stream rushing by. She was cheered to find a couple of granola bars in her jacket pocket, and she munched on one while she searched for more signs of Star.

Losing track of time, Christina was conscious of

only one thing: that she wasn't going to stop until she found her horse. The sun began its descent toward the horizon, and Christina was faced with the fact that it would be dark soon.

"Fine," she said aloud. "Nothing matters except Star."

The next minute, Christina heard a loud crackling noise as a large brown mass hurtled through the bushes next to her.

A bear! was Christina's first thought.

Franky reared up, and in a second he'd dumped Christina neatly on the hard ground. He disappeared in a flash, giving Christina a glimpse of his rounded rump and unshod hooves before he was gone.

Christina sprawled in the dirt, trying to regain her breath as she watched a young deer race past her. His black eyes were huge and fearful, his tan coat mottled. Without pausing to look at her, he leaped into the undergrowth on the other side of the trail, and then he was gone as well.

Dusting herself off, Christina stood up. Surveying the area around her, she fought down another burst of panic. Now she was on foot, armed only with a granola bar, lost somewhere in Montana. It was all too horrible. Star was lost, too, and from the looks of things, they could both die out here and no one would even know where to look for their bodies.

Christina burst into hysterical laughter. At first she wasn't sure how she could be laughing when the situation seemed to be so terrible. But then it came to her: She had to either laugh or sit down and cry. But crying would be like giving up and admitting that she'd lost Star. Better to be crazy than to give up.

With that thought in mind, she stuck out her hand, forced her way into the expanse of bushes that the deer had burst from, and walked in. Branches tore at her face and clothes, but she walked on grimly. There were no more tracks to follow, but Christina moved instinctively, knowing somehow that Star was near. She didn't know why, but she felt it more strongly than she had ever felt anything before.

An hour later Christina emerged at the other side of the bushes, panting and exhausted. Shielding her eyes against the setting sun, she surveyed the panorama below her. Off in the distance she could see some rocky outcroppings and a well. But there was no sign of the ranch house or any landmark that she recognized. Sighing deeply, she sat down on a boulder, took off her boot, and emptied out the twigs and pebbles that had found their way in.

Where would I go if I were Star? Christina wondered. *If only we could read each other's minds the way we used to.* She scrunched up her face and looked up at the sky, trying to put herself in his place.

She began to have visions of herself turning up at Whitebrook without Star. A sob caught in her throat as she pictured Star's empty stall.

"Stop it," she commanded herself, standing up and walking on. Her feet were killing her, but still she pressed on.

Suddenly she heard more crackling branches and the sound of hooves coming toward her. The next instant she was looking straight into a well-loved, copper-colored face.

"Star!" The words seemed to be ripped from her throat as she stood up, half laughing and half crying, to wrap her arms around her horse, who was lost no more.

12

"OH, STAR," CRIED CHRISTINA. "I THOUGHT I'D NEVER SEE
you again!"

She stepped back to look at him silhouetted in the
shadowy darkness. Quickly she ran her hands up and
down his legs, feeling for any puffiness. There was no
sign of swelling or heat, and Christina exhaled in relief.

Reaching up to stroke his muzzle, Christina buried
her face in his mane. She could feel his body tremble,
and she froze as she touched something warm and
sticky—blood! Stepping back quickly, she looked first
at her hand smeared with red, then at the torn blanket
and several small but ragged tears on his shoulder.
Luckily, they didn't appear to be too deep, and Christina could see that the blood had already started to dry
in places.

161

Christina undid the surcingles on the blanket and wadded it up before she tossed it on the ground. She looked Star over again, checking for any other problems that might have been covered by the blanket.

"Thank goodness there's nothing else. Now, if only I had something to clean up those wounds," Christina murmured, peering closer.

The next minute it came to her. As she'd pushed her way through the undergrowth, she had heard the sound of running water. The stream! She would try to lead him over to bathe his shoulder, she decided. But first she had to get him to stop trembling.

She leaned her head against his shoulder, running her hands over and over him, trying to reassure him that she was here and that he wouldn't be alone again. "You're all right now. I'm here," she said soothingly. "I won't leave you." Gradually his trembling stopped.

Darkness descended upon them, and Christina glanced up at the full moon, which was throwing off an eerie light. Instinctively she drew closer to the warmth of Star's body. Overhead an owl screeched and then swooped down almost right on top of them. Christina heard a scuffle as Star whirled to face the noise.

"Easy there, boy," Christina crooned. She continued to stroke Star's neck, considering her dilemma. Maybe Lyssa was somewhere nearby. She could try yelling at the top of her lungs.

Forget it, she decided. She had come a long way from where she and Lyssa had gone off in opposite directions. And what if her shouting caused Star to bolt? She couldn't chance it.

She'd have to spend the night up here and wait till daylight to try to find her way down the mountain. There was no other choice.

Bears, mountain lions, wolves. Mentally Christina ticked off a list of wild animals Lyssa had told her lived around here. She fought down her panic.

"Don't forget the carnivorous kangaroos," she said aloud, smiling wryly. "Lyssa camps out here all the time. Okay, Star, what would she do next?" she asked her horse.

Well, first thing, Christina decided, *she'd get those wounds bathed.* Running her hand along the waistband of her jeans, she confirmed what she already knew: She hadn't worn a belt. She had nothing to lead Star with. How would she ever get him over to the stream?

One thing was for sure—Lyssa wouldn't worry for two seconds about not having a lead rope. In fact, Christina had seen for herself that none of Lyssa's horses needed anything but her voice to guide them. That was because they trusted her implicitly. Up until Star's sickness, Star had trusted Christina like that, too.

Turning, Christina stroked Star's velvety muzzle, trying to focus on his eyes in the moonlight. "What happened to you and me?" she asked. "We used to be so close. Remember?"

Star gave a tremendous sigh that seemed to come from somewhere deep within, and he snuffled her shirt.

Absently pulling a couple of strands of his tangled mane, Christina wrapped them around her fingers and kept talking.

"You see these hairs? Someone once told me that Native American warriors would braid their horse's hair in with their own. It was a symbol that their spirits were one. That was the way we were.

"Remember when we'd fly down the track, and I'd ask for just one more burst of speed and you'd give it to me without thinking twice? And what about when you were slipping away and ready to die? You heard me and you came back. Oh, Star, what happened? What made you decide to leave me?"

The fears and frustrations of the past few weeks poured out of her, and she talked until her throat was dry. Then she fell silent. Lyssa's words suddenly filled her brain.

When Star is sick and hungry and hurt and cold, then he has to turn to you.

Slowly an idea came to her. He was hungry now, hurt and cold. She would turn and walk toward the stream. He would have to follow her. Centuries of instinct would tell him to follow the *itancan*.

Could she trust that he would? Or would she turn and walk off only to have him bolt into the darkness?

She gazed steadily into Star's eyes. "Follow me, Star," she pleaded. "You have to trust me."

Taking a deep breath, Christina turned and started walking in the direction of the water. For a few seconds she heard nothing. Then suddenly the sounds of crunching pine needles and slow hoofbeats reached her ears. Smiling in the darkness, Christina dared to pick up a slight jog and was gratified to hear the one-two, one-two beat as Star began to trot after her.

At the stream Christina put on the brakes, and Star stopped directly behind her. In the moonlight Christina could see that the stream was wider than she'd thought, but, judging by the sandbars visible in the water, it looked pretty shallow.

As she reached her hands into the stream to cup some water, Star snorted and stepped back. There was only one thing to do. Christina climbed on a boulder next to Star and swung easily onto his bare back. Knotting her hands into his mane, she urged him forward, testing the footing gingerly.

Star trembled under her, hesitating. Christina bit her lip and cued him more firmly. Star had to trust her and go forward into the stream. It was now or never.

"Follow me, boy," she murmured just as Star shot into the water, snorting and sending up a splash. Too late, Christina realized that the water was a little deeper than she'd realized, and she gasped as the cold water soaked her jeans to her knees. But Star's feet were firmly planted in the streambed. It was only water, after all.

"It's okay," she said, patting Star's neck. "I'm here with you."

Suddenly Star whirled and plunged, sending up a spray that was illuminated in the moonlight. Christina held on tight as his body twisted and turned. She closed her eyes and felt his body struggling against inner demons that only he could drive out.

"I'm here, Star. I'm not going anywhere," she said again and again, though his whirling and thrashing threatened to send the words back down her throat. "Stop fighting. You're all right now."

It seemed like forever that Christina was thrown around as Star flailed in the water. But just as she began to wonder how long she could hold on, Star's fury seemed to spend itself. Gradually his thrashing lessened in intensity, then finally stopped altogether, and he stood trembling in the stream.

Christina leaned against his neck, shivering in the cold but filled with a warm glow of happiness. Sliding off, she sloshed her way to the edge of the stream. This time, without hesitation, Star followed, nosing her anxiously.

"You're back!" Christina said joyfully.

But she didn't have time to savor the sweetness.

Shivering, Christina plopped her hands on her hips and considered her next problem—how to get both of them dry and warm again. Star's torn blanket was lying in a heap where she'd found him, but there was no point putting it on a wet horse.

She felt in her shirt pocket where she'd stuffed the matches she'd used to light the campfire. They were still dry. Making her way over to a clearing by the stream, Christina formed a fire ring out of some rocks she collected by moonlight, then gathered kindling and small branches. Before long she and Star were looking into the leaping flames of a crackling campfire.

When Christina was sure Star was fully dry, she walked up to collect the blanket. Star followed behind closely, not wanting to let Christina out of his sight. She fastened the blanket on, and they returned to the glowing fire. After a while Christina's eyes felt heavy, and when Star pawed the ground and lay down, she sat next to him, leaning against his shoulder. Finally she slept.

Christina awoke with a start when the sun's first rays broke through the clearing. Wiping the sleep from her eyes, she looked up and saw Star standing over her protectively. The fire had gone out during the night, and Christina stood up, pulling her shirt tightly around her.

Her stomach was grumbling, and Christina thought longingly of the rocks that she'd left up at the station. She wouldn't care if they were drenched in mud. She would wolf them down so fast, she'd beat Melanie's all-time record!

Then she remembered that there was one granola bar remaining in her pocket. Munching on it slowly, Christina looked around and tried to get her bearings. It was time to get out of here and find her way down the mountain and back to the ranch.

"Got any bright ideas, Star?" she asked her horse. "I have absolutely no idea where we are."

Christina poured dirt over the remains of the campfire. Then she pulled off Star's blanket, rolled it up, and set it on his withers. Using a boulder as a mounting block, she climbed onto Star's back behind the rolled-up blanket.

"Well, Star, it's up to you. You trusted me to get you this far, and now I've got to trust you to take us the rest of the way," she said. She nudged him forward but didn't tell him which way to go. Star picked up a brisk walk back to the clearing and started down a path that Christina thought looked familiar. He snorted and arched his neck, and Christina felt the old bounce in his step, something she hadn't felt since before he'd gotten sick at Belmont.

Is it possible? she thought, hardly daring to believe it as they wound their way down the mountain. Suddenly being lost and alone somewhere in Montana didn't seem so bad. She sat lightly on Star's back, enjoying the ride.

Of course, Christina decided a few minutes later, *it kind of defeats the whole purpose of coming here if Star and I get lost in the mountains forever.* Christina squinted and looked for any familiar landmarks. Just then Star's whole body vibrated as he let out a long, shuddering whinny that seemed to echo onto the valley floor.

"What is it, boy?" asked Christina, reaching up to pat his neck. She glanced around, half expecting another deer to come bounding by. But suddenly she heard an answering neigh from just beyond the trees.

Within seconds Lady and Lyssa burst into view, followed by the two geldings.

"There you are!" Lyssa cried, visibly shaken. She looked pale, and there were dark shadows under her eyes. "Where have you been? I freaked when Franky turned up at the station without you. I rode all night looking for you. I only just started back for the ranch."

"Well, then, if you're on your way to the ranch, would you please give me directions? I have absolutely no idea where I am, and Star and I have decided we're getting pretty tired of the great outdoors," joked Christina.

Lyssa studied Christina's face with a raised eyebrow. "All right," she said, placing one hand on her hip. "What's the deal? For someone who's been lost all night, you look pretty well rested—and awfully happy, for that matter."

"Don't you see?" asked Christina happily. She turned out her toes and held up her arms. "Look, Ma, no hands," she said.

Lyssa looked blank.

"I'm riding like you—no saddle, no bridle, no nothing." Christina reached for Star's mane again. "He's listening to me just like he used to. The old Star is back. It's the best thing that's ever happened in my whole entire life."

Lyssa smiled. "I knew it," she said simply.

"You did not!" Christina retorted. It was too much, Lyssa acting as though she knew everything.

But Lyssa didn't say a word. Instead she took Lady over to Star, peering closely at his shoulder.

"How did this happen?" she asked.

Christina looked down at the wounds, which in the daylight didn't look nearly as bad as they had the night before. "Star had them when I found him," she explained. "I think he got hung up on some thorny bushes or something."

"Well, we'll doctor him up when we get back to the Black Thunder," Lyssa said. "It shouldn't be long. The house is right over there."

"You mean this whole time I thought I was totally lost, and the ranch is just over there?" Christina cried accusingly.

"Can I help it if you have no sense of direction?" Lyssa asked, still grinning with relief.

"I guess I owe you big time," Christina said as they headed down to the ranch.

"I didn't do that much," said Lyssa practically. Her eyes swept over the landscape, and she smiled. "And now that Star's back to his old self, we could go on some amazing trail rides. How about it?"

Christina shook her head wistfully. "I hate to go, but Star and I have a lot of work to do before Derby day. We have to head home."

When Lyssa lifted her face, Christina could see that her blue eyes were shining with tears. "But after you and Star win the Derby, you'll come back for a vacation, right?"

Christina reached over and touched Lyssa's shoulder. "You bet we will."

Just then the flat expanse of Lyssa's practice track

came into view. Christina turned Star toward the track. "I think you're ready now, big guy," she whispered. She pressed her knees into Star's shoulders, moved her hands up on his neck, and urged him into a gallop, just like old times. Star leaped forward with a burst of speed.

"Race ya!" Christina called, the cold wind rushing past her ears as Star's powerful strides propelled them toward an imaginary finish line.